This is the anthology you hope to find. Well-written stories engage your interest... to tickle your curiosity and satisfy the need for a quick fiction fix. Well done, Linda.

Donita K. Paul, award winning author. The Dragon Keeper Chronicles.

Cover design by Mercy Wenger and Tabata Catalán
Interior design by Tabata Catalán
Edited by Travis Perry

ISBN: 9798886277111
ISBN: 9781088022337

First edition

DREAMS AND DRAGONS

L. M. BURKLIN

BEAR PUBLICATIONS

This book is dedicated to the memory of my late mother, Donna Jean Moran, who from my infancy taught me to embrace my imagination, to love words, to love stories, and to love the deep music of poetry.

Table of Contents

Sparrow

This story is dedicated to the memory of Matthew Clay Baumgardner

"**M**other," my son said, flashing me his most beguiling smile, "you simply must move in with us now. I agree our current house is a little small, but we've just signed the papers on a bigger place and I know you'll love it. I can afford a nice place now, and we all want you to share it with us."

"I'm fine where I am," I said, but I admit I was curious.

"Just come see it," he pleaded. "You wouldn't even be in the main house with us. There's a guest house—with its own little garden. But you'd be right there on the property with us so you could see us whenever you want. And I haven't even told you the best part yet."

He had just about sealed the deal with the words

"guest house," because I love having my own space, but now I had to ask: "Okay, what's the best part?"

He looked so smug I could hardly stand it.

"Remember that artist you used to talk about when I was a kid? Gard Matthews? The one you said was your friend and then became rich and famous before he died? The one whose work you used to rave about? Remember when you used to say you'd give anything to have a piece by him? Well, I had to fork out a bunch of extra dough to get them to leave the sculpture in the yard for us. Because it's by that guy. Gard Matthews. The previous owners gave me all the documentation for it too, so I know it's authentic. I had it moved to the guest house garden so you'll have it close by."

I had to sit down in a hurry before my knees gave way. I don't know what I had been expecting him to say, but that wasn't it.

My mind wandered back over the years to a time and place I never seek on purpose: the abject poverty of my childhood; the constant exhaustion of my hardworking mother; the string of failed get-rich-quick schemes my father had fallen for; my adorable and needy younger siblings; the persistent hunger. And that night shortly after my fourteenth birthday when I couldn't sleep because my two little sisters kept hogging the blankets on a chilly spring night.

The house was quiet except for the sound of my parents talking as they sat at the table on the other side of the curtain dividing our sleeping area from the kitchen.

"We're going to be on the streets by this time next week if we don't get money from somewhere," Father said. "I know you're working as hard as you can, but that isn't doing much but keeping us from actual starvation."

"Here's an idea," Mother said, sounding more bitter than I'd ever heard her. "How about if you got a real job and earned a real salary?"

"I plan to," he said, "but even if I get hired tomorrow, I won't be paid in time to pay the rent on this dump or pay back my creditors. We need a lump sum in the next few days."

"I don't have any hidden money, if that's what you're thinking," Mother said. "Every time I try to put a little by, you take it and throw it away on one of your harebrained schemes."

I heard Dad pound the table. Any mention of his multiple failures infuriated him. But what he said next made me stop breathing.

"We could sell Lavender," he said. "There are lots of men who'd pay top dollar for a pretty girl like her. She's got that lovely chestnut hair, pale skin and blue eyes—and she's developing very nicely too."

"You can't be serious," my mother said, raising her voice. "Are you suggesting selling your own daughter to some pervert just so you can pay a couple of bills?"

"It wouldn't be my first choice," Father said. "Of course not. But I don't think you understand how desperate our situation is. And the other children are too young to have much value yet. But Lavender . . ." His voice trailed off.

I could hear Mother crying now. "I thought we had a family," she said between sobs. "A family we loved and cared for. But apparently you thought we were just raising livestock that you could sell when things got tough."

"I never thought it would come to this," he said.

"It didn't 'come to this,'" she yelled. "You *drove* us to this! It didn't have to be this way! How dare you talk of selling your own daughter!"

I have always believed my mother yelled on purpose. She hoped I would hear and be warned. I lay shivering and tried to wrap my mind around what I heard.

"Don't say a word to Lavender," Dad said. "I'll put the word out tomorrow and see how much interest there is."

"You may lose more than a daughter," Mother warned.

I lay awake, my mind racing. I loved my family—my mother, my two little sisters and my two little brothers. Despite the frequent beatings, I had even loved my father— or at least wanted to please him. Now the man who should be protecting me was willing to sell me to a stranger—for what? I couldn't bear to contemplate it.

The light went out in the kitchen and my parents' footsteps retreated to the one little bedroom in our apartment. My brothers slept on the couch in the living room. I slid out of the crowded bed, making no noise. Instead of a closet, we girls had a row of hooks on the wall to hang our few clothes. I had been thinking while I waited for my parents to go to bed. I would need to find a job, so I should probably wear my nice dress. I wanted to make a good impression on my future employer. With only moonlight to see by, I lifted down my one "dressy" dress, the one that used to be Mother's, that she had given to me to wear for special occasions at school.

It was kind of baggy on me, and hung almost to my ankles, but it was still a pretty dress and the blue color made my eyes look even bluer. I looked to where my book bag waited on the chair for me to take it to school tomorrow. There could be no more school for me. I slid the books out of the bag and used it to hold a few underclothes, one of my two school dresses, and my pajamas. I put back in my blank notebook and my two pens, because I loved to write.

Last of all, I pulled on my jacket. It was a little tight

and short in the sleeves, but of course we couldn't afford to get one that fit. I looked down at my little sisters asleep in the moonlight. Scarlet, aged eight, and six-year-old Amber. Since our last name was Green, my father thought it would be hilarious to give us all color names. I leaned over and kissed my sisters. I didn't dare cross the kitchen to say goodbye to Browne and Rusty. There was too much of a risk I'd bump into something and make a noise.

With extreme care, I inched the window open until I could duck under it and onto the fire escape. One last time, I looked in on my sweet sisters and blew them a silent kiss, knowing I'd never see them again. I closed the window, then took off my shoes and descended the fire escape in my stocking feet so there'd be no clanging noise. My tears fell in silence also.

On the street at last, I put my threadbare shoes back on and walked away. Not toward the school, which had been something of a haven for me, but in the opposite direction. The city seemed endless and menacing with its colorless buildings and deep shadows cast by the moonlight.

It occurred to me more than once over the next few days that I could be in more danger on my own in the big city than I would be if Father had his way and sold me to some creepy rich guy who wanted a plaything. I tried not to think about it. Often as I walked, tears streamed down my cheeks. I longed to run home for a hug from Mother, to play with my siblings—but I couldn't.

I remembered by the second day that restaurants and grocery stores throw away a lot of still-edible food. After that, I ate better than I often had at home. I walked into shops and small eateries, one after another, looking for work. I said I was sixteen—and I was tall enough for it to be believable. But everywhere I went, I heard, "Sorry, kid. We just don't need anyone right now. And shouldn't you be in school?"

At night I looked for a church and would wander its grounds until I found a bush or shrub I could hide under to sleep, using my bag as a pillow. Somehow I felt safer if I was on church property—until the fifth night of my exile, when it rained. It began as a fine drizzle, but the air was chilly and I was soon damp all over. For the first time, I thought of trying to get inside the church. Tonight's church was a huge old rambling structure—a cathedral. The big front doors were locked, but there were many others. I tried them all, and found them all locked. I thought churches were supposed to be places of refuge!

A flight of stone stairs curled around a rounded tower and led to yet another door. I climbed the stairs and found the door locked like the others. But there was a little roof over it that offered some shelter. I leaned up against the wall as the rain began to fall harder, and scanned the building from my new vantage point, wondering if there might be some other more sheltered spot or an open window somewhere.

A tiny pinprick of light caught my eye. It came from a dingy window high up in the main bulk of the cathedral. Someone was in the building! Maybe they'd let me in. As lightning flashed, I worked out a route to get near the lit window. I'd have to scoot along a roof in a couple of places, and climb up some decorative stonework, but it looked doable to a desperate fourteen-year-old girl who was cold and wet.

I slung my bag over my shoulder, swung my leg over the railing of the little porch where I had sheltered, and set off. Before long I had slipped down a long sloping roof but landed unhurt on a flat part of the roof I hadn't been able to see before. This got me quite close to my goal, and soon I began climbing up the wet stone carvings to reach the dimly-lit window. A rather large fancy shelf protruded right under the window, giving me a place to stand and see if it would open.

The leaded glass panes were grimy and smudged, but I could make out the flame of a candle through them. Lightning flashed again and revealed two things. A person occupied the room, sitting at a table on which the candle burned. And the window was already open—just about an inch.

My hands were numb with cold by now, but I used them as levers to open the window wider until I could climb over the sill and into the room. The man at the table turned and stared at me as the cold wind from the open window struck him.

"Who are you?" he said. "What are you doing here?"

My teeth chattered with the cold. "I just need a place to stay out of the rain tonight," I said. "Can I please come in? I promise I won't cause any trouble."

"You're homeless?" he said.

I realized I was. I hadn't thought of it that way before. I certainly could never go back to my family. I nodded.

"Are you hungry?" he asked. "Because I'm afraid I don't have any food just now."

"Oh no," I assured him. "I had a big supper from the trash cans behind a Chinese restaurant."

He looked a little startled, but didn't say anything critical about my food source.

"My name's Gard," he said. "Gard Matthews. Let's get you warmed up."

He walked over to a pallet on the floor and grabbed a blanket to wrap me in. "Maybe I should look into collecting some wood," he said, pointing at a small fireplace set into the wall. "I've never tried to have a fire but on nights like this it's tempting."

I nodded, wrapping the blanket more tightly around my shivering body.

"Wait here," he said. "There aren't enough blankets

for both of us, but I think I know where to get some."

He went out a door that made a loud creaking sound and I waited for what seemed like a lifetime before he returned. I held my hands over the little tea light candle to warm my fingers.

"Ta da," he said when he returned, holding up some faded brown drapes. "These curtains probably haven't been used in decades, but they were put away clean and in a cedar-lined wardrobe, so they should be okay. And they're lined, so they'll be warm."

The room was long and narrow, up under the eaves of the cathedral. His pallet was at one end, and he made a pallet for me at the other, pulling a row of chairs in front of it to act as a room divider to give me some privacy. While we were setting up my sleeping space, the candle burned out, plunging us into darkness.

"We'll have to finish up by touch," Gard said. "I only allow myself one candle per day. There's no electricity on this level of the cathedral."

Lightning continued to flash often enough for us to see what we were doing every now and then. There were enough of the curtains to drape a couple over the line of chairs, giving me privacy and some shelter from the wind that seemed to blow through the room even with the windows closed.

"There," he said. "It's not fancy, but you've got some padding and the curtains should keep you warm. In the morning we'll have to discuss this situation, Miss . . . Uh, you still haven't told me your name."

I didn't know what to say. If I told him my name was Lavender Green, he might not even believe me. On the other hand, what if my parents were looking for me? What if they had put the word out that a girl named Lavender Green was missing? I couldn't tell Gard my real name.

"I can't tell you my name," I said at last. "It might be

dangerous."

He raised his eyebrows. "Well," he said, "I have to call you *something*. You came in through my window like a bedraggled little bird, so I think I'll call you Sparrow."

"Okay," I said. I kind of liked it.

The next morning we had the promised talk, and I learned many things over some very bitter black coffee that Gard made on a little alcohol burner. Gard was a genuine starving artist. He had found this unused room in the cathedral and was squatting there unbeknownst to the bishop or anyone else, because he couldn't afford an apartment or even a room over someone's garage. No wonder he was so sympathetic to my plight. He showed me stacks of paintings and a few small sculptures.

"I can't believe no one has bought them," I said. "They're beautiful!" In fact they were stunning.

His face reddened. "I haven't actually tried to sell very many," he said. "I struggle with achieving my goals for my art. You say these pieces are beautiful—and to you, they are. But you can't see what I *intended* them to look like. They fall short of what I envisioned because I just don't have enough skill yet. Pretty pathetic for a thirty-one-year old guy, right?"

I shook my head. "It shows you care about quality. But don't forget that no one else can see your original vision either. I bet lots of people would love these paintings and happily pay money for them. Don't ever admit they aren't what you had planned. If you could sell them, you could afford better materials and work on getting better, right?"

He grinned at me. "You're pretty smart for a little sparrow. Maybe you're right." Then a look of concern passed over his face. We were sitting at his worktable in front of the biggest window in the long room. Diffuse morning light flooded the shabby interior and made it look almost homey. He reached out his hand and lightly touched a couple of places on my face, my neck, my arms.

"Bruises," he said. "Who hurt you?"

I hadn't looked in a mirror for months. Hadn't realized I still had bruises from the beatings I'd received on a regular basis.

"Let's just say I can't ever go back to my family. I'm on my own now. I've been looking and looking for a job."

"What a pair we are," he said. "Maybe we can help each other. We'll tell people you're my little sister, if anyone should ask. Now then, Sparrow, how about a quick tour of your new home before people start arriving for morning prayers?"

I stared at him. "I just needed a place to spend the night. You don't have to let me stay here."

"Don't be ridiculous." He grinned. "Would I throw my own little sister back on the streets? Now finish your coffee."

We spent an hour roaming the huge old edifice, poking into storage rooms and rarely-visited private chapels. He showed me where all the bathrooms were. The closest one was two floors down. But there was also a special one for the priests that included a shower. "All the comforts of home," Gard said.

After showing me a much easier way to get to our little domain on the north side of the cathedral, he said, "Sparrow, you need breakfast, and so do I. I just don't happen to have any food, and I spent my last few cents on birdseed, so let's feed the birds before we go foraging for ourselves."

That ledge below the central window that I had climbed on the night before served as a buffet for a variety of little birds, many of them sparrows. Hungry like me.

I watched them, enchanted as they all crowded around the seed we scattered on the ledge. I smiled up at Gard, noticed how skinny he was. "Let me show you how to get food," I said.

He was stunned when I showed him how stores threw away perfectly good food when it reached its sell-by date. The food was still safe to eat for several days after that, I knew. My family had often resorted to food from the grocery store trash when times were particularly hard. We filled my book bag with food and headed back to the cathedral. We had to be very careful about getting back to our room because there were plenty of people around now.

After our hearty breakfast, I looked at Gard. "Now we're going back out," I said.

"Oh?"

"You are going to select a few paintings to sell in the square where all the other artists gather. And I am going to apply for more jobs."

"Who says you can tell me what to do?"

"If I'm your sister I have to help you, Gard. You haven't been helping yourself."

He shrugged. "Have it your way, then. It's worth a try."

Anyone could stake out a few square feet of space and display their artwork for sale. That day Gard sold four paintings to the tourists who thronged the square. When I returned to check on him after coming up empty on my job search, he beamed at me. "We're rich, Sparrow! We're going to have cream and sugar in our coffee tomorrow! And I bought more candles too!"

I heaved a private sigh of relief. The black coffee had been quite a challenge for me. We returned to our room well before dark, feasting on our foraged food, supplemented with some treats that Gard had bought with his earnings.

"How old are you, Sparrow?" he asked.

By now I trusted him enough to tell the truth, at least about this. "I'm telling everyone I'm sixteen," I said. "But actually I just turned fourteen."

He looked at me and to my surprise I saw tears in his eyes. "You poor little poppet," he said. "Life is so unfair sometimes. I had a wonderful family. I wish you did too."

We soon developed a routine. Gard spent the morning painting, because that's when the light was best in our little sanctuary. I washed his brushes and fetched the things he needed, and he talked to me as he worked, explaining everything he did. I never tired of watching him work or listening to him talk.

In the afternoons, we went to the square and I helped him set up under a spindly little tree before going in search of jobs. After only the fourth day of this pattern, Gard greeted me with a very satisfied look on his face. He had sold at least two paintings every day.

"Whenever a rich lady comes to look at my paintings," he said, "I tell them I have a little sister who'd be a perfect household helper. One of the ladies who bought a painting today was interested. She said for you to come to the square with me tomorrow to meet her."

My heart sparked with hope. "I'd better wash my nice dress."

I hated that Gard had to buy food for us both. I wanted to contribute too. So the next day I walked to the square with Gard, scrubbed clean and wearing my spotless blue dress. On the way, I decided to tell the lady my name was Ven Matthews, since Gard had said I was his sister. And Ven was at least part of my real name. Somehow I didn't want anyone but Gard to call me Sparrow.

Mrs. Clay was waiting for us, a tall and rather imposing woman. She had me walk a couple of blocks away with her, to where she had parked her car, and then she drove me to her house. I had a moment of panic, fearing she might live too far away for me to walk, but our route angled back somewhat in the direction of the cathedral, and I realized it wouldn't be too long a walk. No more than a couple of miles.

Mrs. Clay lived in a very grand house, it turned out. Her children were grown and she didn't need a full-time housekeeper anymore, but she did want some help in the house. I assured her I was a good worker and could clean and even cook like a pro. Mostly true. She put me to work and watched as I swept and mopped and scrubbed for four hours.

"You're hired," she said. "But wear some more practical clothes when you come tomorrow. Some jeans maybe."

She handed me cash for the work I'd already done, and told me I'd be working twenty hours a week in the afternoons. Inwardly I exulted because that meant I could still hang out with Gard in the mornings.

I had to spend every cent I'd earned buying myself a pair of jeans and a collared shirt that looked a little more professional than a t-shirt. I couldn't wait to try them on and show Gard. "Do you like my new work clothes?" I asked.

He grinned. "Pretty spiffy. My little Sparrow has practical new plumage now. But I still like your old feathers too." He pointed at my dress, which I'd draped over the chairs making a wall beside my sleeping area.

Over the next few weeks, we both jumped into our new lives. Gard's canvases got bigger and he had a string of profitable portrait commissions. He bought some wood to sculpt, and the scraps we burned in the tiny fireplace so we could warm ourselves and make toast on chilly evenings. I worked every afternoon for Mrs. Clay, cleaning and often cooking supper. She always had me make enough for us both, and I'd take my share home to split with Gard.

The weather warmed up and the hummingbirds came back. Gard loved all birds, but I could see that hummingbirds were his favorite. He showed me how to feed hummingbirds by holding a tiny bowl of sugar water in my hand. He'd made the bowl himself when he'd taken a ceramics course. It was bright red and shaped like a flower. The first time a hummingbird hovered over my hand, I thought I'd die from delight. I loved to stand on the ledge outside the window and wait for the birds to come to me.

In midsummer, when I arrived for work soaked to the skin from a thunderstorm, Mrs. Clay asked me, "Where do you live, Ven? Is it near here?"

I didn't dare tell her the truth. "I have a room near the cathedral," I said. It was kind of true.

"Come with me," she said. She led me up the stairs to the attic on the third floor, which I'd never been asked to clean.

"I've been doing some renovating up here," she said. "It would be so convenient for us both if you lived here in the house, don't you think? And I enjoy your company."

She showed me a modest bedroom with a slanted ceiling, an adjoining sitting room, and a tiny bathroom. The bedroom had a real bed, a dresser, and a wardrobe, and the sitting room had a chair and an ottoman and a coffee table. I had never in my life lived anywhere that nice.

I looked at Mrs. Clay. "Oh, I don't think I can afford it."

"It's part of your salary now," she said. "Think of it as a raise."

To be honest, I was torn. I wanted to live with Mrs. Clay

—but how could I abandon Gard? I thanked Mrs. Clay, but when it was time for me to walk back to the cathedral, I walked very slowly.

"Why the long face?" Gard asked.

I told him.

"But this is wonderful!" he said. "You'll be properly looked after and you'll live in a real house!"

"What about you? Who will fetch your water and clean your brushes and watch you paint and remind you to go to the square?"

He grinned. "You can still do those things—anytime you want. You still have your mornings free, right? You don't get to stop being my little sister just because you're moving out."

I moved into my little rooms at Mrs. Clay's, and over the next month I seemed to find it harder and harder to find time to go to the cathedral and visit Gard. Mrs. Clay found that she needed me more and more. And Gard's life changed too. He had a real bed now, and a propane stove, and the room was beginning to look like a proper artist's studio. "Soon I'll have a real place of my own too," he said.

Then Mrs. Clay fell ill and I was needed to look after her day and night for two weeks. When she finally began to feel better, I asked for the morning off. Caring for her had exhausted me and I missed Gard more and more. In many ways, he had become my family—the kind of family I *should* have had.

I couldn't wait to see what Gard had been working on in my absence. I ran up the stairs and burst into the long room, only to find it empty. Everything had been put back the way it must have been when Gard first found it. There was no sign that anyone had ever lived there.

I sat down in one of the empty chairs and cried my little heart out. How could God take Gard away from me too? The first person who had been kind to me. The big brother I'd never had. I searched the room for a sign that he had left me a note telling me where he'd gone, but I found nothing. No evidence of our months of shared existence.

Heartbroken, I trudged back to my new home feeling like the worst friend in the world. Had Gard thought I didn't care about him? Was I just a nuisance to him, holding him back from what he wanted to do? Was he glad to be rid of me? It occurred to me that maybe a young man in his thirties might not want to be saddled with a needy fourteen-year-old girl.

I never saw him again, not even in the square where the other artists gathered. I scoured the newspapers for word of him. Twice in the next few years, I found announcements of an exhibit at a gallery in the city. Both times I went, hoping to see him. He was not in attendance, but my eyes devoured his paintings and sculptures as if he'd made them for me. I knew him so well, you see. I could hear his voice explaining to me why he'd chosen that shade of yellow for the daisies, or why the little boy was so close to the edge of the pond. The paintings cost more than I could earn in six months. I had no hope of owning one, but how I longed to.

In time, I moved on. Mrs. Clay died and left me enough money to start my own bakery. I met a fine young man, married and had children who were mostly grown by the time I was widowed. I never forgot Gard, though. I tried to honor him by telling my kids about him—the young artist who had taken me in, given me my new life when the old one had shattered. I told them how talented he was, how gifted. And they mourned with me when I found the obituary in the newspaper—Gardner Matthews, artist, dead at 63. I'd never have a chance to look him up, to let him know how well I'd turned out or how much he'd meant to a scared fourteen-year-old girl.

Now my son had bought a house with one of Gard's sculptures in the garden. Could I bear to see it? I wondered if it would have any birds in it. Gard loved birds so much.

As we drove to the new house, I couldn't contain my curiosity. "What's the sculpture of?" I asked.

Matt grinned at me. "It's an angel," he said. "Apparently he was famous for doing a series of angel paintings and sculptures. This one I'm told is called 'The Hummingbird Angel.'"

I nodded. "He loved hummingbirds. He showed me how to feed them from my hand."

"So you've mentioned—a few hundred times. Here we are."

He led me past the big house, through the side yard, and to a delightful cottage surrounded by a lush flowering garden. My eyes immediately went to the sculpture which dominated the round flower bed in front of the cottage.

"I had it face the cottage so you could sit in your house and see it," Matt said. "And I moved a bench so it would be nearby in case you want to sit outside and enjoy it."

I walked closer to inspect the back of the statue. Huge, graceful wings had been carved in translucent white marble. The detail on the feathers made them look real—I almost expected them to flutter in the breeze. The wings hid the angel from behind and formed a sort of informal heart shape.

Standing there, I had a strong sensation of Gard being there with me, right beside me. I could hear his voice saying, "I think I finally got the feathers right. I mastered feathers in paint a long time ago, but stone was so much more challenging. I hope you like my feathers."

Of course I liked them. They were exquisite.

"I can see why you had such a high opinion of his work," Matt said. "Wait till you see the front."

I held on to his arm as we walked around the flower bed to the front. When I saw it, I caught my breath. The "angel" was not what I'd expected. She was a skinny girl—maybe about fourteen years old. She wore a baggy dress that reached almost to her ankles—a dress I remembered well. She had wavy hair and a radiant smile on her face. She held her cupped hands together in front of her. In them was a flower-shaped little bowl, and around it were gathered five hummingbirds, who sat right on the angel's hands. I marveled at the exquisite details on the birds, at the expression on the angel's face which conveyed joy, hope, and delight.

"Didn't I tell you I liked your plumage, my little Sparrow? That lovely old dress of yours will never wear out," Gard's voice said in my head.

"Do you like it?" Matt asked. I turned to answer him and burst into tears. I cried and cried and cried, as he held me tight in his arms. Finally, I pointed at the angel. "It's me," I said. "Me as a girl."

"Are you sure?" He stared at the waif-like angel and then at me. "I guess I can see a little resemblance," he admitted.

Matt's wife Mel ran out of the big house with a large envelope. "I just noticed you're here," she said. "I've brought you the documents that go with the sculpture. We haven't looked at them yet because we wanted you to see them first."

She handed the envelope to me. "Maybe you'd better sit down," my son said, guiding me to the nearby bench, and sitting down beside me so he could read along with me.

The first few papers were sketches that Gard had done

in preparation for carving the sculpture. All of them were of me, all were signed by him, and all had one word at the top: Sparrow. I couldn't stop staring at them. He had seen me, really *seen* me as I was. It was like looking into my own soul as it had been so many years ago: the vulnerability, the fear —and the hope. The final paper was a page from the gallery catalog for the exhibit at which the angel had been originally displayed. It showed a photo of the sculpture, and underneath it the title: Sparrow.

This was followed by the artist's comments: "Although everyone has begun to call this piece 'The Hummingbird Angel,' its true title is 'Sparrow.' Sparrow was a real angel who was sent from heaven on the night I planned to take my own life. She appeared to me as I sat writing my suicide note by the light of my last candle. God knew I needed her more than she needed me. Taking care of her gave me a new purpose and changed my life's direction. I am alive today because of Sparrow, and it's her I have to thank for my artistic success. She knew how I struggled to create in reality the visions I saw in my head. If she were here, I'd tell her that this sculpture of her, more than anything else I've created, comes closest to achieving what I had hoped for."

Matthew put his arm around me as I dissolved into tears again. He leaned closer to give me a tender kiss on the cheek. "Welcome home—Sparrow."

The End

The Mirror

Celeste ran down the forest path toward the river, her breath coming in ragged gasps. Soon her pursuers would be close enough to see her. Without slacking pace, she turned aside from the path and plunged into the undergrowth. So many lives depended on her success tonight, but she'd never been a fast runner.

The footsteps sounded closer now. Celeste burrowed under a dense shrub, ignoring the scratches from the tiny thorns that covered its branches. Struggling to quiet her breathing, she inched forward toward the sound of rushing water. She might not be fast, but she could be clever.

After wriggling on her stomach for a few more yards, she saw it: the river, a road on which she'd leave no footprints. The small ripples in the water gleamed in the moonlight. Could she reach it before she was discovered? A few moments later, she eased her battered body into the cold water and gasped as it sucked the air from her lungs. She fought against her deep desire to relax and drift down with the current. That's what they'd expect. Going that way meant letting them win.

Instead, she swam upstream, pulling herself along the bottom with her hands when the water ran shallow enough.

Her fingers and toes lost all feeling, but she kept going. After what seemed like hours, she reached the shelter of the Greystone Bridge, its timeless arch spanning the river as if it had grown there instead of being built. In the shallows beneath the bridge she pulled her shivering body out of the water and stuck her hands into her armpits in an attempt to warm them. The night air blew on her wet clothes, chilling her further.

As she sat huddled on a rock under the bridge, she realized she was thirsty despite her desperate swim. A puddle of still water gleamed nearby, and she bent over to scoop up some water for a drink.

Before her hands disturbed the surface, it began to glow and she found herself looking not at a puddle in the shadows under the bridge, but at a shimmering mirror which revealed her own face. Her sopping wet black hair framed a thin white face, covered with red scratches and a couple of deeper cuts. Dark blue eyes stared up at her as if asking a question.

Her heart drubbed loudly in her chest. Had she stumbled by accident on the legendary Mirror of Prospect? It was said to appear only to those in extreme peril. She certainly qualified. She tried to close her eyes and found she couldn't. She didn't want to see what the mirror would show her—the moment of her own death. Surely it would occur within the next hour, with her hair still wet and the cuts on her face still bleeding.

But as she watched, her reflection in the mirror changed. The cuts disappeared, the hair dried, and her face began to age. In just a handful of seconds, she found herself looking at an old lady whose face was crisscrossed with wrinkles instead of scratches. The old woman, whom she knew was still herself, looked deep into her eyes and then lay her head back on a soft embroidered pillow. Her eyes fell closed and Celeste knew she was dead.

The mirror vanished and once more she was just an exhausted girl in desperate need of a drink of water and a safe place to hide. Even so, she was not the same girl she'd been even two minutes ago. She was a girl who knew she'd survive her current troubles and live to a ripe old age. There was no question of giving up now. Her mission would succeed, and it would succeed because she was clever and resourceful—and because she knew, just this once, that she couldn't fail.

The End

L. M. Burklin

Cameo

Something sparkled in the grass beside the path up ahead. Despite her hurry, Maggie stooped to see what it was. She reached for it and found a beautiful oval cameo dangling at the end of a fine gold chain. Stuffing it into her pocket, she picked up the pace and jogged the rest of the way to Laura's house.

"Sorry I'm late," she said. "My alarm didn't go off."

Laura smiled. "It's not as if I'm going to sack you if you're late. Sit down and catch your breath while I make the tea."

Maggie sat down at the big kitchen table and set up her laptop next to Laura's, then pulled out the necklace she had found on the path.

"I've got something to post on the Lost and Found message board," she said, holding it up.

Laura stepped over to take a look, and Maggie inspected it for the first time herself. The oval cameo depicted a lovely young girl with wavy hair that was adorned with a daisy chain. The background color was a vivid blue rather than the more common pink or coral.

"It's beautiful!" Laura said. "Where on earth did you find it? A real carved cameo and a gorgeous gold setting. I reckon that's at least fifty years old."

Maggie held the pendant, mesmerized by the delicate image. Her mind raced. Had the carving been made of a real little girl? If so, who was she? How had this lovely piece of jewelry ended up beside a path that ran through cow pastures?

She closed her hand over the necklace and forced herself to focus on the job at hand—updating the village website. She and Laura weren't paid for this labor of love, but they both took it seriously. It seemed, at least to Maggie, that having their own website had brought their little Cumbrian village together. And who knew? Maybe someday there would be a tempting post from an eligible bachelor on the "personals" page.

She pulled up the Lost and Found message board and posted a carefully worded message that she hoped would foil any would-be thieves:

Found: an item of value on the path that runs through the cow pastures of Dickleburr Farm. If you think you might have lost something there, please call or email Maggie McKenzie.

Back home in her tiny cottage that afternoon, Maggie pulled out the cameo again. This time she fastened it around her neck and looked at herself in the mirror. It brought out the blue in her eyes—made her look like an elegant lady. She should have her hair swept up into an elegant bun, and be wearing a flowing silk gown instead of jeans and a rather ragged-looking pullover.

As she stood admiring herself, the phone rang.

"Hello?"

"Is this Maggie McKenzie?" It was a woman's voice.

"Yes, how can I help you?"

"I'm calling about the item you found in the cow pasture. Was it a blue cameo showing a young girl?"

"Yes, you're right. Is it yours?"

"It wasn't exactly mine. I found it too. And if you know what's good for you, you'll get rid of it this instant. Throw it into the river, down a well—anything."

Maggie held the phone to her ear, her mouth hanging open.

"You haven't worn it yet, have you?"

Maggie started. "I'm wearing it now. Just to see how it looks, you know."

A muffled moan came through from the other woman.

"It's too late then. You're doomed, poor soul. She won't let you go, you know."

"Who won't let me go? Who are you?"

There were a couple of heavy breaths and then a click. The phone went dead.

What an odd phone call. Maggie took off the cameo and looked at it. It had a little inscription: to E from G. There didn't seem to be anything sinister about it. After putting the necklace back in her pocket, she settled down by the fire to read and listen to the light rain drizzling in the garden outside. Soon, her eyelids drooped and the book fell out of her hand.

A large meadow surrounded her. Impossibly beautiful sunlight shone on the wildflower-filled field. On the other side of the meadow loomed an imposing mansion.

"That's where you'll find us," said a child's voice beside her.

She turned to look down at an adorable young girl with wavy blonde hair, and her heart skipped a beat. It was the girl from the cameo, wearing a beautiful hand-smocked dress. Her huge eyes were china blue.

"What's your name?" Maggie asked.

"Frances. *He* calls me Fanny, even though he knows I don't like it."

"I don't understand. Who calls you Fanny?"

"Duncan. He's the one that keeps us locked up."

Maggie was bewildered. "Who is 'we?' And why are you locked up?"

"Duncan came and got us after Father died. He wants Mother to marry him, but she says if she wanted to marry him she would have done it the first time. So we have to stay in the house until Mother gives in. You've got to help us, Miss. Duncan said that if Mother won't agree to marry him, he'll hurt me until she changes her mind."

"Oh dear," Maggie said. Her stomach lurched at the thought of anyone harming this sweet little girl. Could this be real?

"You're not in the house at the moment," she pointed out.

France lifted her chin in the air and grinned. "No, but he thinks I am. He doesn't know I can get out the window and climb down the ivy."

"Look," Maggie said, "I want to help you if I can. What is your full name and your mother's name too? Maybe I can call the police."

"I'm Frances Elizabeth Mayhew, and my mother is Elizabeth Agnes Mayhew, but everyone calls her Bess. Quick, sit down!"

Without thinking, Maggie obeyed.

"Why are we sitting?"

"I hear His car coming."

Sure enough, a gleaming blue vintage Daimler rolled past on a gravel road at the foot of the meadow.

"Frances," Maggie asked, "what year is it?"

Frances stared at her as if she were daft. "1940."

Ah ha! This was a dream! Thank goodness!
Frances jumped up.

"I've got to go climb back in before He finds out I'm gone. Please help me, Miss."

Maggie woke with a shiver. The dream had seemed so real. So real, in fact, that she headed straight back to her computer and pulled up the library's genealogy site. She punched in the name Elizabeth Agnes Mayhew.

Elizabeth Agnes Daniels Mayhew: born April 6, 1909. Married Graeme Philip Mayhew June 24, 1929. Declared dead, November 12, 1948. Children: Frances Elizabeth Mayhew, born January 6, 1931.

A chill ran down Maggie's spine. It might have been a dream, but Frances and her mother had been real. And they had been "declared dead?" That sounded ominous. She grabbed her phone and punched in the sequence to call back the number that had last called her. The same voice answered with a cautious "Hello?"

"Did you know that Frances and her mother were real people?" Maggie said without preamble.

"That's not possible," said the voice. "They're just part of a nightmare that never ends. Get rid of that cameo before it ruins your life."

Click.

Without missing a beat, Maggie typed in Graeme Philip Mayhew and pulled up the results. He had been killed in action during the first months of fighting in World War II. Frances had been right. A little more research yielded the information that Graeme had a younger sister and a younger brother. The brother, Matthew, was apparently still alive, though if so, he must be pushing ninety. How could she have dreamed a real story? Time to catch a bus to Carlisle.

An hour later she found herself ushered into a tiny sitting room in an assisted living home outside of Carlisle. Within minutes an old man walked in, leaning on his cane. He had a shock of white hair that stuck out in every direction and twinkling blue eyes.

"Mr. Mayhew?

He lowered himself carefully into the chair beside her.

"How pretty you are," he said. "Why would a pretty girl like you come to visit an old man like me?

"I have some questions about your sister-in-law," she said. "Your brother Graeme's wife."

His bushy eyebrows shot up. "What do you know about poor Bess? Graeme was killed in the early days of the war, you see. Bess and little Frances disappeared shortly afterward and were never seen again. Lots of people thought that she must have gone somewhere out of the way and killed both herself and the girl out of grief, but I never believed that. Bess told me herself that Frances would grow up knowing her father had been a hero and that she had a lot to live up to. I say, you're very pretty. I don't see many pretty girls round here, you know."

Maggie smiled. "And I don't meet many gallant gentlemen either, Mr. Mayhew. I have to ask you something else. Did Bess know a man named Duncan, and if so, what can you tell me about him?"

A cloud passed over the man's face and his blue eyes blazed.

"I suppose you must be talking about Duncan Douglas. The only words I can think of to describe him are not fit for a lady's ears, my dear. His family owned Moorhouse and he thought that plus his title gave him the right to anything he wanted. He wanted Bess, and he might have had a chance with her if she hadn't already been in love with Graeme and if she hadn't seen him whipping his valet for some minor infraction. Bess's marriage to Graeme filled him with rage. He threatened to destroy them!"

"What did he do after Graeme died?"

The old man snorted. "Oh, of course he came slinking back like the dog he was. Begging Bess to marry him. Promising her a life of comfort and luxury. She was pretty like you, you see. But she refused to have anything to do with him. Then she vanished. I think she went into hiding to get away from him."

Maggie let her breath out in a whoosh.

"What if Duncan kidnapped her and held her captive?" she asked.

Matthew Mayhew leaned over and grabbed her wrist. "Now that's just the kind of thing he *would* do. What gave you that idea, young lady?"

She pulled out the cameo and held it up.

"Have you ever seen this?"

"Where did you get that? Graeme had it made for Bess. He gave it to her for her birthday—that last birthday before he went off to the war. That's my niece, little Frances."

"I found it in a field," she said. "I think it's a clue. Where is this Moorhouse?"

"Oh, it burned down in 1942," he said. "Duncan wasn't there, I'm sorry to say. He'd gone off to live in Bermuda and he never came back. But the ruin is still there. Right up near the Scottish border, it is."

Maggie felt sick to her stomach. What had happened to little Frances and her mother? Had they died in the fire? Or were they already dead by then? She'd have to go to the house and look around. She'd have time tomorrow, when it would be Sunday. She'd have to borrow Laura's car.

That night she found it hard to go to sleep. What if she had another dream? She left the cameo sitting on the mantelpiece in the sitting room, even though she found it somehow difficult to let go of it. She built a roaring blaze in the tiny fireplace in her bedroom. Somehow it made her feel safer. Instead of lying down, she sat up in bed with her back against the headboard, her arms wrapped around her knees, her eyes gazing into the fire . . .

She was closer to the house this time, among some trees that grew on the edge of the meadow.

"You said you would help me," Frances said.

Startled, Maggie turned to see the little girl wearing a different dress, and with dark bruises on her arms and legs.

"Did Duncan do that?"

Frances nodded.

"How long since the last time I talked to you?"

"Four days."

"Look, Frances, this is more complicated than you can imagine. When I'm here, with you, I'm asleep. When I'm awake, I'm in the future—the twenty-first century. I have to figure out how to help you and I'm not sure how. Have you and your mother tried to escape?"

Frances gave her a scornful look. "Oh, of course. He sets the dogs on us and then ties us to the bedpost until we promise to behave."

"But you could get away by yourself, couldn't you? Like you have just now."

"I'm not going to leave Mother to that monster."

Maggie reached out to hug the child. "No, of course not. But how far away does your Uncle Matthew live?"

"Uncle Matthew? I don't know. He still lives at home with Granny and Grandfather. He's the best uncle ever."

"Could you walk there and get back before Duncan realizes you're gone?"

A light dawned in Frances' face.

"Yes! During the night—but I'd be scared to go all that way in the dark."

Maggie looked at the sky. It appeared to be late afternoon.

"Look," she said, "if I'm still here when you climb out, I'll go with you. I don't know how long I'll be staying this time—I'm in bed for the night. I have no idea how this works. I don't even know if I'm really here with you in 1940 or if I'm dreaming that I am."

"You seem real to me," Frances said. She held out her arms and Maggie wrapped her in another hug. It *did* seem real. She smelled the sweet little-girl smell of Frances' hair.

Frances took her around to the back of the mansion, hiding behind bushes all the way. She pointed out a block of four windows on the second floor.

"That's our prison," she said. "A bedroom, a dressing room, and a sitting room."

"Listen," Maggie said, "if I'm not here when you come out, that just means I've woken up. If tonight doesn't work out, we'll try again next time, all right?"

Frances nodded. "None of the other ladies even tried to help me," she said.

"Other ladies?"

"The other ladies who came here, like you. No matter how much I begged them, they kept telling me to go away."

The cameo. Other women had found it, had worn it, and had met Frances in their dreams. *That's* what that woman had meant on the phone. Why hadn't they tried to help?

"Look, you'd better get back in before someone

39

notices you're gone," she said to Frances.

She watched as Frances squirmed expertly up the ivy and in through a tiny window that must belong to the dressing room. Who had a dressing room anymore? A little hand waved wildly in the window before disappearing.

A light shone in her eyes. Sunrise. Sunday morning, and she had woken up before Frances could sneak out of the house again. She smacked her pillow in frustration. Why did she care so much about this little girl that had lived—and died—so many years ago? The fire had gone out during the night, and she shivered as she pulled on her dressing gown.

Downstairs, she dialed Laura's number. "I'm coming, I'm coming," Laura said. We've still got plenty of time."

"I'm not talking about church," Maggie explained. "I'm begging you to take me on a wild goose chase after church. I'll pack a picnic if you'll provide the transportation."

"You are making no sense at all," Laura said, "but I'm game for a picnic. Just promise me we won't be doing anything illegal."

Maggie hesitated. "To be honest, I don't know. It's just something I have to do."

After church, they drove out to the village of Hallbankgate and kept going.

"It's not far now," Maggie promised.

"Good, because I'm starving and I demand that you deliver on the picnic before we do anything else."

"There." Maggie pointed to the horizon, where the jagged outline of a once-great mansion bit into the sky. "That's Moorhouse. We can eat now, if you want."

"So why are we here?" Laura asked between bites of

ham sandwich.

"I want to look around that house. I've heard it's abandoned, but I still didn't fancy coming here alone."

"What do you think you're going to find?"

"I don't know. Some answers, I hope."

"And you're not telling me the questions, I gather?"

"Well, not yet. You'd never believe it anyway."

She fingered the cameo in her pocket. She felt she should have it with her on this excursion. They finished eating and then drove past what had once been a meadow but was now dotted with trees and shrubs. The overgrown gravel drive even sported a few small shrubs.

Laura grunted. "You didn't tell me we'd be off-roading it."

"I didn't know. Until we got here, I wasn't even sure the house existed. Drive around to the back, okay?"

Laura pulled up behind the house, near what must have been the kitchen door. They got out and looked around. Some of the roof had fallen in. The right side of the house, the side that Frances and her mother had occupied, showed heavy fire damage. The other side just looked rather sad and derelict.

"Now what?" said Laura.

"Well, I suppose we go inside."

"Are you sure it's safe?"

"No."

"What are we looking for?"

"I don't know."

The two of them stepped around plants and pieces of rubbish that littered what had once been a paved terrace. The kitchen door gaped open, and they instinctively held hands as they crossed the threshold. The kitchen, which must have been impressive back in the forties, had since served as a home to various forms of wildlife.

"We need to see if there's a way to get upstairs without risking our lives," Maggie said.

Laura shuddered. "This is the creepiest place I've ever seen. You'd better have a top-notch explanation for all this."

Maggie led the way out of the kitchen and into a hallway. The ground floor appeared to be quite sound structurally. They passed rooms with ruined tapestries and velvet curtains hanging in ribbons. A magnificent set of stairs appeared at last, but the top third had fallen in. Laura wanted to leave, but Maggie refused to give up.

"A house this size is bound to have more than one staircase," she said.

They backtracked to the center of the house and started exploring the side that had the least damage. Sure enough, a second set of stairs appeared, much less grand than the one they had already seen. They looked sound enough.

Maggie stepped onto the stairs and proceeded upward, testing each step carefully before putting her whole weight on it.

Laura stood at the bottom with her hands on her hips. "I'm not coming up there with you."

Maggie shrugged. "All right then, you just stay there and wait for me."

A moment of silence ensued.

"I'm not staying here by myself!" With a grimace, Laura followed Maggie up the creaking stairs.

Upstairs, sunshine came in through holes in the roof and illuminated the wide hallway. Maggie's curiosity got the better of her and she started opening doors to see what the rooms looked like. Most were once-opulent bedrooms or sitting rooms. She did not venture into any of them until she came to a very masculine-looking bedroom on the left side. A picture on the mantel caught her eye and she tiptoed into the room to get a better look while Laura dithered in the doorway.

Maggie picked up the tarnished silver frame and blew the dust away from the picture. The black and white portrait showed a beautiful young blonde woman dressed in the "flapper" style of the late 1920's or early 1930's. She had multiple strands of pearls hanging from her neck and large, penetrating eyes. Maggie turned the frame over and carefully extracted the old photo to look at the back, where a brief inscription read: *Bess '28.* Maggie felt as if she'd been punched in the gut. Not only were the people real, but she now had proof of Duncan's connection with Bess. She replaced the photo in the frame and carried it with her back to the hallway to show Laura.

"Who is that?" Laura asked.

"Bess Mayhew. Now we've got to see if we can get to the other end of this hallway."

"Why?"

"Because that's where he held her prisoner."

"You must be mad."

"You may be right."

They inched down the hallway on tiptoes. There were some soft spots in the middle, but next to the walls the floor seemed quite firm still.

"How do you know where to look?" Laura hissed.

"You wouldn't believe me."

To their left, the "front" half of the house was a burned-out shell. Whole walls were missing. To the right, the walls were blackened but still standing. They reached the last three doors left on the right side. The first gaped open and showed what seemed to have been a linen closet. Maggie shuffled to the next door and turned the handle, pushing as she did so. The door fell inward with a resounding WHOOM, causing both girls to jump.

Inside the room stood a burned and blackened canopy bed and a partially-burned dressing table with its tarnished mirror. To the left, an open door connected this room to the sitting room beyond. Maggie saw that much of the sitting room floor was gone, and sunshine poured into it from the huge holes in the roof. Her breath came in gasps.

"Did the lady in the picture live here?" Laura asked.

"Not willingly."

Maggie turned and looked at the right wall. There was another door there, this one closed. She knew it must lead to the dressing room, the one with the little window Frances had climbed out of.

"I've got to see the dressing room," she said. "You don't have to come with me."

"No, I'll stay right here and have my phone ready to call for help when you plummet though the floor."

Maggie sidled around the perimeter of the room. After reaching the corner intact, she turned left and inched toward the door, reaching gingerly for the doorknob. She almost expected it to still be hot after seventy years. The knob turned, and pushing the door open, she held her breath.

The dressing room showed smoke damage, but didn't seem to be as burned as other rooms they had seen. Maggie tested the floor in front of her and took a step. Straight ahead on the other side of the room an open door showed the bathroom beyond. To the right, a U-shaped clothes rack full of clothes filled the space. Ladies' clothes filled most of the rack, but little girls' clothes hung on one side. Maggie crept over to the side with the girls' clothes and looked through them. One of them, a light blue dress with beautiful smocking across the chest, was the dress Frances had been wearing the first time they met. She lifted it off the hanger.

The fragile fabric was stained with smoke, but the dress was still recognizable. Maggie hugged it: a tangible connection to the girl in her dream.

Turning toward the tiny window that looked out over the back garden, she saw a chair in front of it, and a large wooden wardrobe on either side. She sidestepped back past the doorway and made her way to the first wardrobe, pulling the doors open.

"What on earth are you looking for?" called Laura. "I want to get out of here!"

Glamorous evening gowns filled the wardrobe. Silks and satins, fur and sequins. They were all fabulous. Maggie fought the temptation to grab an armful of the vintage gowns and take them home. After closing the wardrobe, she moved to kneel on the chair and look out the window. Ivy covered almost every square inch, but she could see the back garden through the gaps, and the strip of forest where she had hidden to wait for Frances.

With a sigh, she turned to the other wardrobe. The doors seemed to be stuck. She gave the handle a vigorous pull, and the whole room creaked and shifted. Laura shrieked, and Maggie bit her tongue to keep from doing the same. Bracing her hand on the left side of the wardrobe, she pulled again with her right. The door sprung open. Maggie opened the left side too and looked inside. Elegant silky nightgowns and dressing gowns hung on the rod. Thinking she saw something in the back right corner, she cautiously pulled the garments aside.

A sound somewhere between a sigh and a groan escaped her.

"What is it?" Laura yelled.

"I found them," she said. Two skeletons crouched in the corner, one with its arms wrapped protectively around the other. They must have died of smoke inhalation. Maggie stood and stared. She didn't feel fear or horror. Instead, hot tears rolled down her cheeks and her chest heaved with sobs. That sweet little girl! She covered the bodies again and closed the wardrobe doors.

Still holding the photo and the dress, she picked her way back to Laura. "They're both dead," she said. Laura's eyes almost popped out of her head.

"Who? Who's dead?"

"Bess and Frances."

They picked their way back to the stairs and down to the kitchen. Still weeping, Maggie stopped dead in her tracks when she saw someone waiting outside by Laura's car.

"May I ask why you two ladies have disturbed the peace of Moorhouse?"

An elderly lady gazed at them with piercing black eyes.

Maggie swallowed, trying to quell her weeping. She had been caught red-handed. She still held the picture and the dress.

"I was looking for proof that Bess and Frances Mayhew had been held prisoner here, and I found it," she said.

The older woman's face changed the instant she heard the names.

"Aye, they were held here all right, poor things," she said. "My mother was the housekeeper here, you see. Young Frances was about my age. I tried to befriend her, but every time I was caught talking to her I was punished."

"Why didn't someone let them out during the fire? I found their bodies up there, in the wardrobe."

The old lady sighed. "You found them? Oh, what a shame. That was a sad business, that fire. It's my belief that Lord Douglas set it himself. He tired of waiting for Mrs. Mayhew to submit to his desires."

"But I heard he was in Bermuda at the time of the fire!"

"Oh, no, lassie. That's what he paid the staff to say.

When the fire started, he ran down the stairs telling everyone to get out. He said the Mayhews had already been taken to safety."

Tears glinted in her eyes.

"That lying bastard. He stood on the lawn with us watching the house burn, not lifting a finger to stop it, and then he drove off in his big blue car before the firemen arrived. We never saw him again. I suppose he really did go to Bermuda then."

"Why didn't you tell anyone about the Mayhews?"

"Oh, I did, love. But you must remember, I was just a wee child and all the adults contradicted me. They were that afraid of Lord Douglas, you know. I still come here of a Sunday afternoon and ask God to forgive the wickedness that went on here. I'm glad you found the truth. Do you suppose we can get a proper burial for that poor lady and little Frances?"

"I think we can arrange something. I'll ask Matthew Mayhew about it when I see him again."

The truth was, Maggie hoped she could somehow stop the fire from happening. She remained silent during the drive home, despite Laura's nonstop barrage of questions.

"Look," she said when they had reached her house and gone inside for a cup of tea, "I don't know what to tell you. It started with that cameo I found. It belonged to Bess Mayhew. I had to find out what happened to her. I . . . I feel responsible for her and little Frances."

Laura shrugged. "Well, are you going to report the bodies?"

"Not yet. There's something I have to do first."

That evening, Maggie rummaged through her bathroom cabinet until she found the prescription sleep aid left over from when she had her wisdom teeth out. Once again, she built up the fire in her bedroom. This time she wore the cameo around her neck and laid the dress and the photo in her lap after she propped herself up with pillows.

"Please, God," she prayed, "let me stay long enough to help."

The setting sun sank behind the black bulk of Moorhouse. For the first time, Frances did not appear as soon as Maggie did. Maggie shivered a little as she got into place behind some shrubs that bordered the kitchen garden. She watched the ivy as the dusk deepened into twilight and then night. Now she couldn't see a thing except the lights in the kitchen windows and a few others. The lights in the Mayhews' quarters were on also.

After what seemed like forever, the lights in the upstairs bedroom went out. A few minutes later, a dim light appeared in the little dressing room window. Maggie glimpsed the silhouette of a head and shoulders before the light went out. She stood up, every sense on alert. Then she heard the pattering of little feet on the grass.

"Frances!" she whispered.

The footsteps stopped. Maggie whispered again. "It's me, Maggie."

A faint whisper came back. "The nice lady who wants to help me?"

"Yes."

A moment later she wrapped her arms around Frances' lithe little body. The girl had the sense to wear a warm cardigan over her thin cotton dress.

As the two of them walked hand in hand along a path

through the woods, the moon rose golden and enormous, as if eager to light their errand. Maggie picked up the pace.

"Are you sure you know the way to your grandparents' house?" she asked.

Frances gave an exasperated sigh. "Everybody knows where my granny and grandfather live."

They walked on in silence for over an hour. The rising moon illuminated the lane where they walked and made the stone fences gleam like silver.

"Are we getting close?" Maggie asked. She was almost dragging Frances along now. Probably the only exercise the kid got was climbing up and down the ivy.

"There it is!" Frances pointed.

They were on a rise and Maggie saw a tiny village nestled in a depression some half a mile away. Much closer a large mansion gleamed in the moonlight, one with a much friendlier profile than Moorhouse, at least in Maggie's prejudiced opinion. Now it was Frances who ran and pulled Maggie along.

"That's Uncle Matthew's room," she said, pointing to a pair of dimly lit windows on the second floor. "He's probably still up studying because he's sitting his O Levels in a few weeks."

She giggled. "Let's surprise him."

After retrieving a key from under a flower pot, she led the way through the servants' entrance and up a back staircase to a door on the second floor. Grinning at Maggie, she knocked loudly.

"I'm just going to bed, Mother," a male voice said.

"I'm not your mother," Frances said in her clear, little-girl voice.

A crash sounded within, and then the door was thrown open by a rather scrawny teenaged boy with dark hair that sprouted from his head like a fountain.

"Franny!" he said, scooping her into his arms. "My

little snapdragon, my apple blossom! Where on earth have you been all these months?"

Then he lifted his eyes and saw Maggie. His jaw dropped, and he lowered Frances back on to her feet.

"And who's your very attractive lady friend?"

Maggie offered her hand in greeting. "My name is Maggie and we need your help and we may have very little time."

He waved them into his study and listened as they told him an abbreviated version of the whole story.

"So you see," Maggie explained, "we need you to help us rescue Bess right now, tonight."

Matthew looked at Frances, whose bruises were only too evident in the light of his study lamp.

"I can't take on Duncan by myself," he said.

"You don't have to," Maggie replied. "I think I've got it sorted out. Is there someone else you can call on to help?"

"MacGregor!" Matthew yelled.

A trim, impeccably dressed man in his forties appeared as if by magic.

"This is my valet, MacGregor. He was a hero in the last war, and he's still better than any two other men. He'll help if I ask him to."

"All right," Maggie began. "I assume you can drive, Mr. MacGregor?"

"Yes, ma'am."

"Well, you two must drive over to Moorhouse—as close as you can get without being heard. Then climb up the ivy to the dressing room window. It'll be a tight squeeze, but I think you can both make it. Get Bess to hide in the dressing room while you stand guard in the bedroom.

"Frances and I will stay here and give you, say, half an hour before we call the police. When the police drive up to Moorhouse, Duncan will try to hide or hurt Bess, and that's what you've got to prevent, right? So barricade the door and have some weapons handy if he manages to get in before the police do."

"And then," Matthew said, "if it all ends well, we return triumphant and you agree to marry me, right?"

Maggie laughed. "You're too young for me now, Matthew, and the next time I see you, you'll be too old."

"I am not too young!" he said. "How old are you anyway?"

"Twenty-five. And don't you know it's rude to ask? Now get going."

"Can't I come too, Uncle Matthew?" Frances gave him a pleading look.

He knelt down and looked her in the eye.

"Now look here, my little mango tree," he said, "I'm counting on you to send the police to rescue your mother and me and MacGregor. Remember, according to your heartless friend here, she could disappear at any moment."

Frances hugged him. "Don't let Duncan hurt mother," she said.

"If Duncan lays a finger on her he'll wish he'd never been born. And that's on top of what he'll get for touching you."

Maggie hugged Frances and moments later watched as the car rolled quietly out to the road and turned toward Moorhouse. She looked at the grandfather clock. 1:47.

"Frances," she said, "when the clock says fifteen past two, we've got to wake up your grandfather and get him to call the police. I think it will be taken more seriously if he makes the call."

She sat on the settee and Frances climbed into her lap. One by one, they watched the minutes tick by.

"Why do you think you found me in your sleep?" Frances asked.

"It's the cameo," Maggie explained. "I found the cameo with your picture on it, and then bang! Every time I fell asleep I found myself with you."

The little girl's eyes lit up.

"It worked! Mother prayed and prayed for a way to let people know where she was. Then she got the idea of having me drop the cameo outside near the back drive of Moorhouse. She hoped someone would find it and wonder who it belonged to and why it was there—and that it would lead them to Duncan. There have been ever so many ladies who have come here like you, you know, but none of them would help us no matter how much I asked."

"Well, I suppose it's a good thing *I* eventually found it," Maggie said.

The clock chimed once for the quarter hour. Frances leapt up. "I'm going to get Grandfather."

Maggie followed her down the hallway to another door, and Frances pounded on it with her little fist.

Maggie awoke in a room flooded with sunshine. Her gaze flew to the clock on her bed stand. She was already late for work. She kicked her legs in frustration. Not now!

The minute she got off work, she called Laura.

"Laura," she said, "I need to go back out to Moorhouse. Can you please take me out there?"

"What, now?"

"Yes, now. I don't know how it turned out. I don't know if the grandfather called the police. I *have* to know, Laura."

"Well, *I'm* not going out there again. You can borrow my car, but I'm not going with you. It's creepy. And there are dead people there."

Half an hour later Maggie was on her way to Moorhouse in Laura's car. She had been able to think of nothing else all day. She got quite a shock when she turned off the road and on to the drive that led to Moorhouse. The drive was paved and well-kept. The flower-filled meadow held a couple of cows that gave her thoughtful looks as she drove past. Then she looked ahead to the house and stomped on the brakes so hard her head hit the steering wheel.

The house had vanished. There was no sign of Moorhouse as she'd seen it only yesterday. In its stead she saw a much smaller, much more modern-looking house made of grey stone, and surrounded by colorful informal gardens. Maggie sat there for a few minutes, trying to take it in. Well, she had to know. She drove forward again, and pulled up in front of the attractive stone house.

After getting out of the car, she walked to the front door on shaking legs. She clutched the cameo in her hand, not sure why she had brought it.

The door was opened by a very tall, very handsome young man with sandy hair and laughing green eyes.

"Maggie!" he said. "So you've come at last!"

He shook her hand vigorously, his large mouth grinning from ear to ear. She had never seen this man in her life. Who on earth could he be? And how did he know her name?

"Granny!" he called. "It's Maggie! She's come at last!"

"I'm Gerald, by the way," he said, as he ushered her into a comfortable sitting room. "Granny will be here in a moment."

Maggie heard the tap and shuffle of approaching feet and then a spry old lady came into the room. She had snow-white hair and bright, china-blue eyes. She held out her hands to Maggie.

"Maggie! How lovely you look. Just like I remember you. I've been waiting ever so long to thank you, my dear."

Maggie gaped at her.

"It's me, Frances," the old lady said. "You helped me escape from Moorhouse and rescue my mother."

"Then your grandfather made the call and the police went to Moorhouse?"

"Yes, yes, thanks to you. When Duncan realized he was well and truly trapped, he shot himself, thus saving the government the expense of a trial. Uncle Matthew and MacGregor were the heroes of the day and we all agreed it would be too hard to try and explain your involvement, so we didn't."

"But what happened to Moorhouse?"

"Oh, you see, I knew you would come back here someday. Looking for me, of course. So Uncle Matthew and I talked my grandfather into buying the place for my mother and of course she had that hateful house torn down as soon as the war ended and she had remarried. She built this house in its place—a house of joy instead of sorrow. Gerald here is my grandson. He's been staying with me while working on his dissertation, and I've told him all about you and how pretty and resourceful you are."

Maggie's cheeks grew hot and she found herself unable to look at Gerald.

"Uh, Frances," she said, "I've brought you something. It's yours, anyway."

She pulled out the cameo and placed it in Frances' hand. The old lady gasped.

"Mother's cameo! You've kept it safe all these years."

Maggie laughed. "No, I've only kept it safe for a few days," she said. "And I can't tell you how glad I am to be able to give it back to you!"

Frances put the chain around her neck and fastened it before giving Maggie a warm hug.

Maggie clung to the old lady, her eyes filled with tears of relief and gratitude. Frances was alive and happy after all these years! A weight had been lifted.

"You simply must stay for supper," Gerald declared. "I make a killer beef curry and I could use some help in the kitchen."

That night when Maggie went to sleep, she didn't dream about Frances at all. Gerald, however, had a starring role.

The End

The Jade Dragon

S omething in the apothecary's booth caught Korik's eye that morning. It wasn't a thing he had seen. It was the absence of a thing.

"What happened to the jade talisman?" he demanded. "The one carved as a dragon pouncing on a snake?"

The apothecary stared back at him with her pale blue eyes.

"I sold it," she said. "This is a shop, you know. My job is to sell things. That talisman was particularly powerful."

Korik suppressed a snarl. Of course it was powerful. That was why he had spent the last seven cycles saving up to buy it. With the power of that talisman, perhaps the Trakken Lord could be swayed to let Korik wed his daughter Lorsa. Now, he'd lost his chance.

"Who bought it?"

Maybe it was someone who could be bargained with.

"That information is available—for a price."

"You are a sadistic and greedy necromancer," Korik said—but he paid her price.

"Your brother Trist bought it," she said. "Perhaps it is a gift for you. He knew you wanted it. The price was high."

Korik ran away from the booth, into the town, and

soon pounded on his brother's door.

Trist opened the door and stepped aside to let him in.

"You knew I wanted that dragon!" Korik yelled. "It was my only hope for persuading the Trakken Lord to let Lorsa and me get married!"

Trist gave him a rather odd smile.

"Come in," he said. "You are welcome here."

That smelled ominous, but Korik crossed the threshold nonetheless.

Trist indicated they were to sit on either side of a small table which held the exquisite jade carving.

"What's going on?" Korik demanded. "You want me to sit here and envy you for having what you knew I wanted?"

Trist shrugged.

"Did it ever occur to you," he said, "that you might not be the only son of our house who loves the daughter of the Trakken Lord?"

A weighty silence seemed to stretch on for years. Korik's heart pounded in his chest until he feared it might burst. He had never dreamed his own beloved brother might be his rival for Lorsa's love.

"Because I love you both," Trist explained, "I petitioned the talisman to unite Lorsa with the man she loves most. I would not want her to be unhappy. If it is you she loves, I will not stand in the way. If she comes to me, however, I expect the same from you."

Korik didn't hesitate. With one swift motion he drew his dagger and thrust it into his beloved brother's heart. With Trist dead, Lorsa would have to come to *him*.

He was still cleaning his knife when Lorsa's maid burst through the door.

"My mistress is dead!" she wailed. "She was coming here, to this house, and she fell dead in the street!"

Korik stared at the girl as he tried to absorb what she said. He ran out into the street and saw Lorsa's lifeless body lying just a few feet from his brother's door. He picked up her limp body and carried it tenderly into the house, where he laid it next to Trist's body. Tears streamed down his face as he kissed both of his loved ones for the last time.

This, the talisman had done. Since Lorsa had loved Trist, and Trist was dead, the only way for her to unite with him was in death. Korik had been a fool. He had killed the two people he loved most, destroying their dreams and his own chance for happiness.

Rising from his knees, he picked up the jade dragon and hurled it against the wall, where it shattered into innumerable pieces.

The End

L. M. Burklin

The Hand of Luriel

Torin Ironwood shaded his eyes as he looked through a gap in the snow-covered mountains. He began to think his mission was pointless. If the fugitive Vex Vinland had indeed fled this direction, at this altitude, surely he must have frozen to death by now. Torin rubbed his mittened hands together. He had never been this far north or this high up into the mountains, and would not be here now if it weren't for the fact that Vex had taken a priceless artifact with him.

Sighing and shivering, Torin continued along the side of the mountain. The sooner he found Vinland—or his body —and recovered the Hand of Luriel, the sooner he could be on his way home to his village in the faraway foothills.

A few steps later he lost his footing on some loose gravel hidden beneath the snow. One foot shot out from under him and he had no time to catch himself before he fell headlong down the mountainside. He lost consciousness on the way down. Eventually he came to a stop covered in snow, and awareness returned.

He couldn't see his body under all the snow, but he knew he had broken a leg. Unbearable agony shot through his nerves. Even so, he clamped his mouth shut to keep from screaming and giving away his location to Vinland. Flinging his bruised arms around, he was able to shake most of the snow off his body. His right leg was bent at an unnatural angle. Rolling carefully, moaning with anguish, he succeeded in straightening his leg out a little. The pain of that effort caused him to pass out once again.

When he opened his eyes, it was midday and the weak winter sun glared off the snow. A shadow fell across him and it took him a moment to realize that there were no trees on this mountainside. He wasn't alone. Had Vinland found him?

Taking a deep breath, Torin looked toward the shadow's source, expecting to find himself on the sharp end of a sword. Instead, his eyes met those of a pale young woman clad in white fur. Wisps of white hair escaped from her hood, and her eyes were such a light shade of blue they were almost colorless. He tried sitting up to greet her, but fell back in pain, unable even to speak.

"Are you hurt?" she asked. Her voice was low and musical.

He nodded, keeping his eyes on her.

"Can you walk?"

With extreme care, he shook his head slightly.

Without breaking eye contact, she gave a sharp whistle and he heard rustling in the snow.

"Snowflake, Blizzard," she said. "Keep him warm while I go for the sled."

Torin heard panting and then two white faces looked down at him. Faces belonging to snow wolves, the wolves of the far north. They were said to be merciless predators. These two, however, looked at him with their deep golden eyes and then lay down. One stretched across his feet and legs, and the other on his torso, breathing warm air on his face. The weight of the wolf was not as painful on his leg as he'd expected—no doubt because his leg was already going numb from the cold.

The woman nodded. "I will return as soon as I am able."

Torin looked up at the wolf which lay on his chest. "Never thought I'd be glad to see a wolf," he said. The wolf licked his face.

Despite his living fur blanket, Torin's chill increased and he faded out again. He regained consciousness when he felt himself being jostled.

"Anything you can do to help me will increase your chance of survival," the girl said. She had pulled a long flat sled up beside him and was trying to roll him onto it. With a massive effort, he threw himself sideways and ended up mostly on the sled, gasping with pain. The girl and her wolf friends worked to get him straightened out and strapped down. Then she harnessed the wolves to the sled and they began to run. She ran beside the sled, encouraging them.

Torin had lost all track of time and didn't know if the journey took mere minutes or much longer. After a while, they passed under a deep overhanging rock, and then the girl held some sort of covering aside while the wolves pulled the sled right into a room with a crackling fire. She released them at once and they lay down on the hearth, panting.

The girl knelt down beside Torin. "You know your leg is broken?"

He nodded.

"I will attempt to splint it, but I'm sure it will hurt. I will warm some spirits for you to drink, and perhaps that will ease the pain."

She warmed a colorless liquid in a pot over the fire, then poured it into a ceramic cup for him to drink. He sniffed it. "What is it? It doesn't smell like any drink I've ever had."

She almost smiled. "It is made from ground-up cones of the spike conifers that grow in some of the valleys around here. I make all my own spirits. It comes in handy for medicinal purposes. Now drink it down."

The drink was strong and had an aftertaste rather

reminiscent of tree resin, but Torin drank it without complaint. The process of setting his leg which followed was even more painful than he had feared, and he almost bit through the rolled-up piece of leather the girl had given him to bite down on. The leg had broken in two places.

When it was over, she helped him roll off the sled and sit in front of the fire with his legs in front of him and pillows behind his back. His right leg was very bulky, wrapped in thick wrappings and braced with wooden slats of some sort. The girl sat in a fur-covered low chair on the other side of the fire, the only seat in the room.

She had taken her furs off, and for the first time he got a good look at her. The white hair provided a startling contrast to her young face.

"Your face is young but your hair is so white," he said.

She returned his gaze without even a hint of a smile. "It turned white from sorrow, not age."

"And your eyes—how pale they are! Yet still beautiful."

"I wept all the color from my eyes some years ago."

He stared at her. So very beautiful, yet she almost seemed to emanate sadness. "May I ask your name?"

"My name is Wynter. At least that is what I call myself now."

"And I am Torin Ironwood," he said. "Forgive my curiosity, but why are you so full of sorrow, Lady Wynter?"

Her head drooped. "I live a cursed life."

His heart went out to her. So young, and already cursed! "What is the nature of your curse?"

She stood up and turned her back to him as she did something on a table near the wall of the cave. "You might say I am cursed with loneliness," she murmured.

He breathed a little easier. That didn't sound too dire. "Perhaps I can keep you company for a time," he responded. "I won't be able to move around much for a while anyway."

Her pale sad eyes sought his once more. "You will not stay long, Torin Ironwood. My loneliness is very cold."

He watched as she heated up some stew over the fire, and gratefully ate the portion she offered him. Afterward, he helped as much as he was able to turn the sled into a comfortable bed with cushions and furs. The two wolves lay in front of the fire watching his every move.

"If you require assistance in the night, you have only to call my name and I will hear you," Wynter said. She disappeared behind a leather curtain on the far side of the cave. One wolf followed her, but the other remained watching Torin with its golden eyes.

Wynter sat on her bed and looked down at Snowflake. Had she broken some kind of rule? If what she said was not allowed, she shouldn't have been able to say it. Part of the curse was that she could not tell anyone its true nature. Loneliness was a *consequence* of the curse, for sure, but the curse itself doomed her to a life in the mountains of the far north. If she were ever to venture to a place where she could not touch snow, her faraway parents would die, and so would she.

Not for the first time, she wondered if it would have been so terrible to marry the sorcerer who had sought her hand. He might have been old and grouchy—but he was also rich and powerful. She would have lived in his luxurious mansion with servants at her command. Perhaps in time she would have come to care for the bitter old man. Instead, she and her parents had politely declined his offer, and this curse on them all had been the result. Her parents had to live far away south in the tropics. If they ever saw snow, Wynter would die and so would they. For six years this reality had ruled her life. She could not leave the snow and her beloved parents could not come near it.

As she snuggled down under her furs, she thought of her guest, Torin. Why had he ventured so far north and up into the mountains? He had been bold to do so. Could he perhaps help her discover a way to break the curse? No, of course not— because she was forbidden from telling him the truth.

Over the next couple of weeks, Torin tried to make himself useful. Clever with his hands, he eagerly mended and made things for his melancholy hostess. She brought him a pair of forked branches that he was able to fashion into crutches, making it much easier for him to get around her cave dwelling. His leg remained painful, and he wondered how useful it would be in the future. Always, at least one of the wolves watched him, and he speculated about whether it was to protect him or to guard against him somehow. Maybe both.

He had been with Wynter for sixteen days before she said, "We have so few visitors this far north. What brings you to my frozen domain?"

There was no reason not to tell her. "A hunt," he said. "Though by now I'm sure the trail is cold, and I have failed."

"What do you hunt?"

He looked into her sorrowful eyes. "A man. A man who stole a valuable artifact from our village, after we had managed to keep it safe for over two hundred years."

"It must be valuable indeed."

He nodded. "So I've heard. It is used as a last resort. It's displayed on certain feast days, but I've never seen it used."

"What does it do?"

He shrugged. "Who knows?" This was not technically a lie, since it was a question. It occurred to him that if she knew of the Hand's power, she might want it for herself, and his sworn quest was to return it to his village unharmed. To the best of his recollection, the Hand had only been used once in his lifetime, when the earl had been wounded killing a boar which had been raiding the village gardens. The healer had done what he could, but it was clear the injury was fatal.

The Hand had been brought forth in great ceremony and carried in its carved box into the earl's big house. Torin had no idea how it was used, but the earl recovered quickly and was back on his feet and telling jokes to the village children within three days.

Wynter broke into his thoughts. "How big is this artifact? What does it look like? Perhaps my wolves and I can search for it while you recover."

He sighed. "I've never seen it close up, but it's the size of a human hand, because that's what it is."

Her eyes widened. "A hand? Severed from a body?"

He nodded. "The hand of Saint Luriel, who was martyred over two hundred years ago. I heard that the flesh turned to stone, but as I said I've not had a good look at it myself."

A look of relief washed over her face. "So, it's not bloody or rotten?"

"Just frozen, I assume."

"Of course," she muttered, "if it was still flesh it would be much easier for my wolves to find."

Over the next week, Wynter was gone for hours at a time, leaving one wolf with Torin and taking the other one with her. When she returned each day, she shared the details of her fruitless search, and he marveled that she never seemed to be discouraged.

"I haven't had any real purpose in so long," she said. "I look forward to the search each day. Thank you, Torin Ironwood, for giving me something to look forward to."

He looked at her sad, beautiful face and thought he had something to look forward to also—her company and his conversations with her. Having grown accustomed to his presence, she often asked him questions about the outside world. He told her about his village and his family and about his one amazing journey to the city of Seahaven, on the coast, where the king lived.

She, however, was not forthcoming when he tried to find out more about her. She commented that her parents lived in the far south and she hadn't seen them in years— but she didn't say why, nor explain why she continued to live alone in such a harsh climate.

Three weeks after his injury he began sneaking out of the cave when Wynter was gone, exercising his injured leg and training himself to walk with the splint on, despite the excruciating pain. He suspected that the bones were not healing quite the right way, and resigned himself to a lifetime of limping. Perhaps he might continue to need a crutch or cane. Soon the winter weather would become even more severe, and it might not be possible for him to return home. He had mixed feelings about that prospect. Despite her continued melancholy, he felt drawn to Wynter. Would it really be so terrible to spend a few months here if he had her to keep him company?

A week later, as he limped back and forth in front of the cave, he felt a surge like lightning in his injured leg. The sensation passed almost immediately, but left his leg feeling strong and whole. Perplexed, he tried taking a couple of steps without even a staff to lean on. His leg felt as good as new. Shouting with joy, he lurched across the snow for a couple hundred yards, with Blizzard bounding beside him. Incredulous, he removed the wrappings and splint from his leg and tried standing again. It was as if he'd never been injured.

It hadn't snowed that day, and he could clearly see the tracks that Wynter and Snowflake had left when they departed that morning. "Let's go meet them!" Torin said to Blizzard. "Won't they be surprised?"

Less than half an hour later Blizzard howled and then rushed ahead of Torin. Looking forward, it took him some time to make out the movement of white on white that was Wynter and Snowflake. He ran toward them. As he approached, Wynter stood still, with a wolf on either side of her.

"You seem to have made a miraculous recovery," she said.

"Yes! I don't know what happened but suddenly my leg was completely healed! It doesn't even hurt at all."

"I also had a successful day," she said. "Snowflake and I found a dark-haired man frozen to death under an overhanging rock. I took the liberty of going through his things and I found this."

She reached into her furs and pulled out a carved wooden box that Torin had seen on several occasions. He sucked in his breath. "Did you open it? Is there anything inside?"

In response, she undid the clasp and opened the lid. Inside the velvet-lined box was a gray stone hand. It was slim, as if it belonged to a lady. The hand of Luriel!

Wynter closed the box and offered it to Torin. "Your quest is complete," she said. "You can return to your village before the worst of the winter sets in."

"Yes," he said. "Yes I can."

That night, when Torin finally went to sleep with the box right beside him, he had a strange dream. Blizzard the wolf lay in his usual spot before the fire, but he began talking to Torin.

"You cannot abandon my mistress," he said. "She will die of loneliness."

"I don't wish to leave her," he said, "but every time I've suggested that she could come with me, she has refused."

"And yet she clearly enjoys your company," the wolf said.

Torin wouldn't have used the word "enjoy." He had yet to see Wynter smile even once.

"What does the hand do?" the wolf asked.

Torin paused. "I guess it performs miracles, if you know how to ask it," he said.

"Do you know how to ask it?"

Torin shook his head.

The wolf yawned, showing its sharp white teeth. "I think breaking a curse would count as a miracle," he said, "just like healing a broken leg."

Torin gasped in shock. What an idiot he was. Of course she must have somehow used the hand to heal his leg. Instead of using it for herself.

He woke with a start. The fire had burned low and Blizzard lay in front of it, staring at him as if trying to continue the dream conversation. Torin sat up and threw a couple of logs on the fire.

"I'm just going out to get some air," he said. Throwing on his coat and boots, he stepped out into the freezing winter night—and he took the box with him. Stars spangled the sky from one horizon to the other. Blizzard had followed him and stood in front of the leather door-flap to the cave, watching.

Torin opened the box and then set it down in the snow. He lifted out the stone hand, surprised at how heavy and warm it felt. The hand was open so that if Torin held it in his right hand, it would be as if he shook hands with the long-dead saint. He gripped it and held tight.

"Saint Luriel," he said quietly. "I am not worthy of your help and I don't ask anything for myself. I don't know the nature of the curse on my friend Wynter, but I ask you to remove it. Heal her sorrow. Bring joy into her life."

For a moment, the hand was so soft he had the sensation he was holding a real hand of flesh and blood. Then it returned to hard stone, though still warm. He replaced it in the box and closed it, stuffing it back inside his coat. How would he know if anything had changed? Would Wynter even know if the curse was lifted?

As he looked out over the snow-covered mountains toward the south, a pillar of fiery light shot straight up from the ground to the sky. It burned brighter than a thousand bonfires for maybe as long as a minute before vanishing upward into the sky.

"Did you see that?" Torin asked Blizzard. "I've never seen anything like that before."

He turned to go back into the cave, only to almost run into Wynter, who had come up behind him.

"What are you doing up in the middle of the night?" she asked.

"I might ask you the same thing."

"Let's go in and get something hot to drink," she said.

He followed her inside, where she tossed her coat onto her chair before reaching for the pot to warm some sweet sap she harvested from trees that grew farther down the mountains. She set the pot on the fire and then grinned up at Torin.

It took a moment to register. She smiled at him! She stood and stepped toward him. "Have you guessed yet?"

As he watched, the pale blue of her eyes darkened to the color of the deep blue sea. Her hair became streaked with gold until the white disappeared completely. A healthy pink glow came up in her cheeks. She was even more beautiful now than before.

"The curse?" he asked.

"Gone," she said.

"Does that mean you can come with me to my village?"

"I would love to see your village."

He cleared his throat. "If we are to travel together, it would be more acceptable if we were married."

She laughed, a sound he had never heard before. "Are you proposing to me, Torin Ironwood?"

He grinned. "Are you accepting my proposal, Lady Wynter?"

She stepped into his arms with a mischievous smile. "Don't call me Wynter anymore," she said. "My real name is Sunflower. And soon it will be Sunflower Ironwood."

They began their hike southward the next day, with the wolves pulling the sled piled with Sunflower's possessions. Late in the day, they passed a valley marred by an ugly black crater that contrasted with the pure white of the snow. Sunflower paused, and grabbed Torin's arm.

"I had to know for sure," she said. "That is where the sorcerer lived. That fire you saw in the sky must have been this place burning."

Torin shuddered. He had no idea he would unleash that kind of destruction when he asked for help for Sunflower.

She smiled at him. "Come on. We're only a couple of hours from the village where I grew up. I bet there's an elder there who could marry us."

Almost three weeks later, the two of them walked wearily into Torin's home village. Since it was the middle of winter, even here the snow was more than deep enough to support the sled as the wolves pulled it. Villagers stopped and stared at the sight of tame snow wolves—and Torin with a girl. His little sister Anya was on an errand of some sort when she saw them. Instead of running to hug him, as he expected, she ran screaming toward home, yelling, "Torin's back! And he's got a girl!"

That evening, after a warm reunion with his family, Torin and Sunflower walked through the snow to Elder Gasthar's house. When the elder opened the door, his eyes lit up. "You have kept me in suspense for hours, young man," he said. "I heard you had returned, and I must know if you were successful."

Torin pulled the box from his coat and presented it to the elder. Then he took a deep breath. "I have a confession to make. My wife here was under a curse. I did not know the nature of the curse, only that it made her very sorrowful and lonely. I . . . petitioned the hand to break her curse, and my petition was granted. If I have done wrong, please tell me what I can do for penance."

"I also," Sunflower spoke up. "Torin was severely injured, so it was actually I who found the hand. I hated for him to be in pain, and trapped in the mountains, so I petitioned the hand to heal him—and my petition also was granted. If Torin must be punished, then so must I."

Torin stared at his new wife. He knew she must have

used the hand to heal his leg, but this was the first time she'd admitted it. Hand in hand, they faced the elder.

Elder Gasthar beamed at them both, then burst out laughing. "Don't look so anxious," he said. "The two of you hit upon the hand's secret without being told, and lived to tell the tale. How can I punish you for that?"

"The secret?" Torin asked.

"Yes, the hand has a secret. Saint Luriel was a kind, compassionate and generous woman who thought only of serving others. Shortly after my predecessors realized the hand had power, they learned the hard way that the hand only grants petitions that are for someone else—and it punishes the selfish. If you, Torin, had asked the hand to heal you, you would have died. And if you, Sunflower, had asked the hand to lift your curse, you too would have died. This is why we guard it so carefully. It will not grant a selfish petition. I would venture to guess that the thief Vex asked the hand for something for himself. But you two—each of you thought only of relieving the other's pain. Go in peace, live a life full of love and joy—and may you continue to put each other's happiness before your own."

The End

Green Meadows

Tara Mull took a deep breath as she climbed the steps to her mother's front door. Every encounter felt like a battle these days. She rang the doorbell and when Mother opened it, her first words were, "So I see you decided to show up after all. Come to gloat over my misfortune, have you?"

"No, of course not, Mother. I've come to help you pack for Green Meadows." She stepped into the cluttered front room of the modest house.

"I wouldn't have to pack if you and your brother had done right by me," Mother said.

Tara didn't rise to the bait. The decision had been made. Her brother, Arthur, lived hundreds of miles away and had a busy life with his wife and five children. He didn't have even an extra square inch to offer his mother. And Tara's job required almost constant travel overseas. Mother needed to live somewhere she'd be looked after, somewhere she could get help if needed. Better to do it now before she had a nasty fall and broke her hip. Assisted living was really the only option—but downsizing from a house to a single room would not be easy.

The morning consisted of almost constant bickering

and a fair amount of packing. Mother didn't want to let go of anything, and Tara retaliated by sneaking bags of junk out to the dumpster when Mother was distracted by something else. Right before lunch, Tara pulled a box down from a closet upstairs and opened it, finding several old photo albums and dozens of loose photos. She carried it down to the kitchen.

"Look what I found," she said. "Photo albums from when Arthur and I were kids."

Mother's eyes lit up. "Let's look at them while we eat lunch. I'd forgotten about all those old albums. Don't even think of tossing those into the dumpster."

Tara winced. She had no intention of tossing them. Instead, she hoped to scan them all and share them with her brother. Opening an album at random, she found it full of photos of her childhood—pictures of her and Arthur as little children, of their parents looking so young and glamorous. She turned the pages one by one as she and Mother exclaimed over the memories.

She came to a section filled with photos of a beach—her and Arthur in swimsuits, building sandcastles, looking for seashells. "Do you remember that?" Mother asked. "That's the time we went to the coast on our vacation. You were only five. You almost drowned, you know."

Tara gazed at the landscape and the ocean waves, trying to remember. "What happened?"

"Arthur threw a fit because I wouldn't let him have an ice cream cone, and while your dad and I were trying to calm him down, you ran off and jumped into the water. Of course you didn't know how to swim. By the time I realized you were gone and stood up to look for you, you had gotten into deep water and were slipping beneath the surface. There's no way I could have reached you in time."

Staring at the photos, Tara strove to dredge up a memory of that long-ago trip. She turned the page. There.

That man looked familiar. The photo showed her and her mother, with her mother clinging tightly to her little girl, but off to the side stood a long-haired, bearded man in dripping wet cut-offs and t-shirt, with a big grin on his face. Tara pointed at him. "That's the guy. He saved me, didn't he?"

Mother adjusted her glasses and scanned the photo. "I don't know, to be honest. Some young hippie jumped in and grabbed you and brought you back to me. He never told us his name and was gone before we could thank him properly. Dad must have taken this picture because we were so glad to still have you. That *could* be your rescuer, but you have to understand I was more focused on you right then."

Tara studied the photo for a few more moments. Who was this man who had saved her life? He seemed to be of average height and build. He looked like every other hippie she'd ever seen.There was nothing at all remarkable about him, yet thanks to him she hadn't died at age five. "Thank you," she whispered.

A few minutes later they came to photos of another vacation, this one in the mountains of Colorado. She remembered that trip well. She had been nine. "Almost lost you that time, too," Mother said. "Dad was trying to get you to pose in front of a guard rail and you and Arthur were goofing off as usual. You leaned too far back and went headfirst out into space. Four hundred feet straight down, and yet somehow you managed to fall on top of a climber who was securely roped, and he caught you."

Tara examined this new set of photos. One of her and Arthur posing in front of the guard rail at the scenic overlook, making silly faces. She remembered the terror of losing her balance and tumbling over the guard rail—and right into the arms of a strong young climber a few feet down. "Whoa there, Missy!" he'd said. "You're supposed to stay on the other side of the railing."

He'd carried her up to the overlook and handed her back to her horrified parents. She remembered his smell— like pine needles—and the red bandanna tied around his ponytail. Ever since that day she'd been terrified of heights. She flipped the page and found a photo Dad had taken of Mother hugging her fiercely after her rescue. In the background, walking out of the frame almost, was her rescuer.

A thrill of recognition shot through her body. She grabbed the previous photo album and flipped to the photo of the man who'd rescued her from the water. "Mother," she said. "I think it was the same guy."

She looked from one photo to the other. In the first photo he was bearded, and in the second clean shaven, but the resemblance was striking. Mother grabbed the two books and looked from one to the other. "I can see a similarity," she said, "but there's no way it's the same guy. That's ridiculous. There are thousands of brown-haired guys like that in this world. The two locations are hundreds of miles apart."

After working with her mother all day, and dreading the thought of having to return tomorrow, Tara dragged herself home that evening, taking the whole box of photo albums with her. Ridiculous as it seemed, she was on a mission. She made herself a mug of hot chocolate and started going through all the albums they hadn't looked through during their lunch break. By the time she became too sleepy to keep looking, she believed she had found five more photos of the same man. He always appeared in the background of photos in which she was the primary subject. Most were taken during family vacations, but one was a snapshot she'd sent her parents of a concert she'd gone to while in college. In that one the mystery man was dressed as a security guard and had very short hair. Although the photos were taken over a span of several years, the man never seemed to age.

Tired as she was, sleep eluded her as she considered the unknown man. On the one hand, it seemed kind of creepy that some guy had been stalking her basically her whole life—yet at the same time, he had saved her life on at least two occasions. She owed him her very existence. Her last thought before falling asleep was, "I'm going to find that guy and thank him. If he's still around. And then I'll ask him why he can't leave me alone."

Helping her mother pack and move filled the next several days. The constant criticism wore Tara down, and she found herself snapping back, only to see her mother dissolve into tears. "I'm sorry, Mother," she said. "I know it's hard to have to leave your home after so many years." Privately, she realized that when this time came for her, there would be no dutiful son or daughter to help her pack and ease her transition. She'd be on her own.

That final afternoon, Tara left her mother in Green Meadows, comfortably ensconced in her new room with all her favorite things around her. Tears slipped down Tara's cheeks as she left the building. Why did Mother have to be so awful about everything? Why would anyone want to visit such a grumpy old lady? She would call Arthur when she got home and vent to him about it. He was always a sympathetic listener.

Lost in her thoughts, Tara moved forward to cross the street when the light turned green, only to be forcibly jerked back by someone grabbing her left arm. "No suicides here, please," said a deep voice, as a delivery truck ran the red light and zoomed right over the spot where Tara should have been.

Tara turned to look at her rescuer. It was him! The man in the photos. "You!" she said.

He gave her a puzzled look.

"That's the third time you've saved my life," she said. "Thanks so much. And who the heck are you? Why do you keep following me around?"

He shrugged as he released her arm, and flashed her a disarming smile. "I don't know what you're talking about," he said as he turned away. But as he strode down the sidewalk, she could have sworn she heard him mutter, "at least a dozen times, but who's counting."

She definitely planned to tell Arthur about this too.

Five years passed, and Tara made a point of visiting her mother at Green Meadows whenever she happened to be in town. She always kept her eyes open for the mysterious man, but hadn't seen him again. Her visits to Mother were depressing and demoralizing. Mother always berated her for not coming often enough and for not staying long enough and for not being married. Nothing ever seemed to be "enough" for her.

Now, Mother had begun to fail. She seemed shrunken and frail, a shadow of her former robust self. Her almost-transparent skin revealed a network of large blue veins. Tara sat beside her wheelchair and wondered if this might be the last time she saw Mother alive. Part of her looked forward to a future when she didn't have to come to Green Meadows every time she was in town, but mostly she struggled with regret.

As if hearing her thoughts, Mother spoke. "I know you think I'm a grouchy old lady," she said. "And you're right. But you want to know why I'm grouchy?"

Tara sighed, bracing herself. "Why are you grouchy, Mother?"

"I'm grouchy because I raised two beautiful kids and now I hardly ever get to see them. I'm grouchy because I have the smartest, most beautiful daughter in the world and her employers don't value her like they should. And apparently the only men she's met are half-baked half-wits who can't see what a catch she is. I'm grouchy because I'm stuck in a stupid wheelchair and I can't take my amazing daughter to museums and plays and fancy restaurants like I always dreamed of doing. I'm grouchy because everything hurts and nothing works the way it used to. Most of all, I'm grouchy because I know every time you walk through that door, your visit will be too short and I'll say something to hurt your feelings, even though I don't mean to. Then I will cry when you leave—and you know how much I hate crying. You probably think we've had plenty of years together—but they're not enough. Not anywhere near enough. You and Arthur are what I live for, Tara."

Tears rolled down Tara's cheeks as she looked at Mother, at the watery blue eyes staring back at her, filled with a mute entreaty. Mother had never spoken to her like this before. For the first time in Tara's life, she considered that maybe the many things that Mother had said and done, the things that had driven her absolutely crazy, had been said and done out of love. She thought back to her childhood and saw certain incidents in a new and different light. So many times when Mother had yelled at her, it had been out of fear for her safety—not out of some sort of innate hostility. The woman who criticized and clung was a mother who adored her only daughter, who wanted the best for her and who wanted as much time with her as possible.

Tara smiled and patted Mother's hand. "It's a beautiful sunny day," she said. "How about if I push you in your wheelchair around the garden outside? You've always loved being outside."

An orderly opened the door as Tara pushed Mother out. He looked vaguely familiar, but Tara was focused on Mother and didn't give him a second thought as she breezed past him and inhaled the lovely scent of pine.

The sunshine glinted on the water in the fountain as Tara and Mother made their way around the garden on the wide smooth paths. Tara told funny stories of her travels, and Mother told funny stories about Tara as a child. Laughter rang out over and over again. It was by far the best visit they'd had in years. At some point during the conversation, Tara realized the bitterness she'd harbored for so long had somehow dissolved. She forgave her mother for all the things she'd done—all the things Tara had been holding against her. Love was better—so much healthier than resentment. Even the sunshine seemed brighter.

When Tara wheeled Mother back into the building and to the dining room to join the other residents for supper, she leaned down and hugged Mother's frail body; planted a kiss on the maternal cheek. "I love you so much, Mother," she said. "I'll be back tomorrow. In fact I think I'll postpone my next trip so I can just hang out with my favorite old lady for a few days. I've got plenty of vacation time coming."

Mother made a dismissive gesture with her hand. "I know how boring this is for you. You don't need to stay around on my account."

Tara shook her finger. "I kind of think I do. See you tomorrow, Mother. Now don't go having any wild parties without me."

Tomorrow, as it turned out, was too late. Mother suffered a fatal stroke during the night, and when Tara arrived first thing the next morning, the body had already been removed. She sat down in her mother's room, on her mother's empty bed, and for the first time, she really saw her mother's home. The walls covered with photos of her and Arthur at every age, and photos of Mother and Dad, with and without the children. The lopsided doily Tara had crocheted in seventh grade, proudly displayed on a side table. The misshapen ash tray Arthur had made in school for his nonsmoking mother, who used it as a ring holder. The photos of the grandchildren, and Tara posing before various world landmarks. The basket full of letters and postcards that Tara had sent. They looked worn, as if they had been read and refolded many times. Her mother's words from the day before rang in her head. "You and Arthur are what I live for, Tara." How had she not seen it, all these years?

Sitting in that empty room, she sobbed alone. An orderly who must have heard her as he walked past the open door came in and gently patted her back. "It's okay to be sad," he said. "Sadness just means that the person you've lost was precious to you. Someday you'll be grateful you had someone you loved so much that her passing broke your heart." Somehow, even over the sound of her own weeping, the voice sounded familiar—and comforting. But when she looked up to thank the man, he had already left the room. Only the scent of pine remained—probably some kind of disinfectant.

Eventually she recovered her composure enough to call Arthur. Somehow, they had to plan a funeral in the next few days. It wasn't fair. After all those years spent resenting her mother, they'd only had that one wonderful afternoon together. Mother had been right. It wasn't enough.

Several months later, Tara traveled to the Swiss alps for business. Determined to conquer her fear of heights, she rented a car and drove up to a mountain pass where she could drink in the sublime alpine landscape and think about how Mother would have loved to see her photos of it. On the way back down the mountain, two things happened. Her brakes failed, and a flock of sheep poured into the road ahead as she hurtled down much faster than was safe.

Desperately she jerked the steering wheel to the right as she tried to avoid the sheep. The car crashed through the guard rail and over a precipice, rolling many times before coming to a stop in a green meadow at the bottom of the incline.

Tara lay stunned for a moment, surprised at how little pain she felt. "Let's get you out of this car," a voice said in English. Strong arms pulled her out of the window, which had been open to let in the fresh mountain air. She found herself lying on a patch of grass, looking up at a man whose features she couldn't see because the sun shone so brightly behind him. The scent of pine needles perfumed the air.

"I'm not sure I can get up," she mumbled.

"I'll help you," he replied. He knelt down and lifted her gently to a sitting position. Now she could see his face. Her mystery man.

"You!" she said feebly. "Why didn't you stop me from crashing?"

He smiled and pulled her to her feet. "Because your time has come and because you've forgiven your mother," he said. "I couldn't let anything happen to you until you made that choice. I wanted you to feel the freedom of forgiveness."

She shook her head, trying to clear it. "Who are you? Why have you been following me around my whole life?"

He lifted her chin and stared into her eyes. "I'm what you might call your guardian angel. It's been my job to

84

follow you around and keep you safe. A very challenging job, I might add." He grinned.

"Oh? What about today?"

"Today I'm more of a *guiding* angel. My job is to take you home, Tara. Look."

She followed his gaze and stared down at her broken body lying on the green grass in the bright alpine sunshine. Tears sprang to her eyes. "I'm dead?"

He put his arm around her. "Oh no, Tara. You're more alive than you've ever been. You just don't need that body anymore. Let me take you home. You're going to love it."

The End

L. M. Burklin

Meredith

Clutching my locket in my hand, I surveyed the idyllic scene. "I made it, Mom," I said. One of the few things I'd taken from home was my mother's silver heart-shaped locket. Inside, a wedding photo of her and Dad filled one side, and a photo of me and my siblings the other. Having them with me comforted me, and I talked to them all the time. It's not like I had anyone else to talk to. Everyone I ever cared about had died.

I wiped the sweat from my forehead and grinned at the beautiful green valley with a small lake at the bottom. Several cabins clustered around the lake, but I doubted anyone lived there. Over the last year, a pandemic had wiped out ninety percent of the world's population. Most cities had become ghost towns. My hometown had emptied except for gangs of thugs who roamed around looting and plundering all the empty homes and stores. I had to find a safer place to live—and I hoped, to grow up. At sixteen, I had a powerful desire to live, even in this bleak new world.

Over the next few hours, as I explored the valley, I discovered that some of the cabins had been designed to operate without electricity, and all were unlocked. I found many oil lamps, and propane gas-powered fridges and freezers still full of food. I had to assume the stuff in the fridges had gone bad, but the freezer stuff should be okay if the gas hadn't run out.

I had hiked several strenuous miles on this warm summer day, and as I inspected an overgrown vegetable garden, the lake caught my eye. I strode down to the dock and sat down to take my shoes off. Lowering my sweaty feet into the cool water, I savored the peaceful feeling that washed over me. I had never felt more safe.

Something grabbed my ankles. Grabbed and *pulled*. I wrapped my arms around the mooring pole to my right and held on tight, kicking my legs frantically. I tried to see what had me but with all the splashing I couldn't tell. I braced myself for losing one or both of my feet.

Then, the grip loosened and my feet flew free, showering me with water. I pulled them onto the dock. A laughing face appeared in the water in front of me.

"Okay, you win," she said. She appeared to be about my own age, bare chested, with wavy black hair. Then I saw the tail, shimmering like a rainbow trout. My mouth fell open in shock. A mermaid? In a lake in the Smoky Mountains? I struggled with words.

"Uh, I'm Emma. Why did you try to pull me under?"

She tossed her wet hair. "Well, *Emma*, it's a game I play to protect my valley. You're the first person who's beaten me."

I stared at her in horror. "You've *killed* people?"

"They had no right to swim in my lake like it belonged to them. The people that really own it are all dead. Why aren't *you* dead?"

"I have a genetic anomaly that makes me immune to the plague. The rest of my family didn't make it. I hope this valley can be my new home."

Her expression softened. "So you're an orphan, like me."

I nodded.

"To be honest," she said, "I'm pretty lonesome. I might let you stay if we can be friends. But it won't work as long as *he's* here."

I had to ask. "Who's *he?*"

"I don't know his name. He never comes to the lake. He's got a gun and he hunts a lot. He shoots anyone he finds in this valley and he'll shoot you if he sees you, so the first thing you've gotta do is get out of sight."

Panicking, I looked for cover. A couple hundred yards down, huge bushes hung over the edge of the lake. I sprinted for them and wormed my way in. My murderous new friend swam to my hidden location.

"What's your name?" I asked, when her faced popped out of the water.

She laughed. "You couldn't pronounce it. But the people who used to live here called me Meredith."

"Okay then, Meredith, how am I gonna be able to stay here if there's some guy out there wanting to shoot me?"

She sighed. "If you could lure him into the lake I could totally take him. But I don't think he likes the water."

I shuddered. "No, I've got to figure out a way to get him on land. Do you think I could negotiate with him? Maybe agree on territories or something?"

She shook her head. "You'd be dead before you could even suggest it. I'm telling you he shoots everything that moves. It must be pretty bad out there in your world."

"There's not much of my world left," I admitted. "But I sure would like to stay in this little part of it."

"Well, he lives on that side somewhere," she said, pointing to my left. "Not in one of the cabins you can see from here. It must be farther up."

I waited in my uncomfortable refuge until late in the afternoon, when I saw a man walking on the far side of the lake. I watched as he rounded the end of the lake and turned uphill. My whole body relaxed—at least a little. Now I knew where my opponent was and that made it easier to keep him from finding me. He appeared to be a man in his forties, maybe, with a pronounced limp. He carried a gun under one arm, and a dead dog hung from his other hand. Did he plan to eat the dog? I tried not to retch in disgust.

I pulled out my locket and opened it. "Dad, I need your help right now," I said, staring at the tiny photo of my parents. "I don't want to kill anyone but if I don't, he'll kill me. I wish you could be here to help me."

As I crawled out of the bushes into the twilight, I remembered how Dad always said, "When you're not sure what to do, don't rush into anything. Observe for a while and see if you can figure out what action you should take."

Meredith swam beside me as I walked. "What are you gonna do, Emma?"

"I'm going to observe him for a while," I said.

"Okay, but watch out for the bears."

Bears? There were bears? Of course there were. No doubt their numbers had increased with the disappearance of most of humanity.

The tiniest kernel of an idea popped into my mind. "Hey, Meredith—are there any fish in that lake?"

Just enough light remained for me to see her roll her eyes. "What do you think I eat, dummy? There are thousands of them in here. That jerk up there never goes fishing."

"So you're pretty good at catching them?"

"Duh!"

I grinned. "I might need your help before long."

As I tiptoed up the path I'd seen the man use, my mind filled with doubt. What if that man and Meredith were in cahoots? What if she helped him by sending victims his way? What if I was walking into a trap?

A couple hundred yards along the path, I stopped. I hadn't explored this far earlier, and if I had, I never would have felt safe. Next to the path an area had been leveled, possibly for a garden of some kind, but now it served as a graveyard. Instead of stones there were just boards with crude writing on them. "White woman April 3. Cherokee man May 12. Teenage white boy May 23." I counted nine graves. Maybe Meredith had told me the truth about this guy. In my head, I started calling him "Killer."

I began to step very carefully, grateful the moon had already risen and provided enough light for me to see the trail ahead of me. After tiptoeing through some trees, I emerged in a clearing with a modest log cabin. Light gleamed from the bare windows. I inched closer, until I could look into the kitchen and watch Killer skinning the dog carcase.

I turned as I heard a snuffling sound on the other side of the cabin, then held my breath as an enormous black bear waddled out of the forest, its head raised as it sniffed the air. I didn't dare move, but the bear seemed focused on the tempting smells coming from the cabin and never even glanced in my direction.

The bear pawed at the door. "Leave me alone, you stupid bear," yelled Killer. "I don't want to waste a bullet on you. I've got plenty of meat right now."

The bear nosed around on the porch before shambling back into the forest. I waited until it had time to get well away before hightailing it back down to the dock. Meredith appeared almost instantly.

"I see you're still alive," she said.

"Alive and inspired," I replied, "and I'm going to need your help."

After telling her my plan, I hiked over to a cabin where I'd seen some burlap sacks, then hauled them to the lake. All night Meredith brought me fish to put in the sacks, a few at a time. It took hours to stuff four sacks with fish. I couldn't fill them to the top because then they'd be too heavy to carry.

In the dim light before dawn, I dragged my sacks up the trail one by one, so thankful Killer didn't keep a dog as a pet. I suppose he was too mean to feed it.

As quietly as I could, I spilled one sack out on and in front of Killer's porch. The others I doled out a few fish at a time in straight lines leading from the clearing. By the time I finished, dawn was approaching and I smelled like fish. Did I go rinse off in the lake? Heck no. Several of the cabins had outdoor water pumps and I used one to douse myself thoroughly, shivering in the cold air.

I let myself into a cabin near the lake, where some of the windows looked out over the trail leading to Killer's cabin. Sitting down in a corner, I hoped Killer wouldn't see me if he happened to look in my direction. I smiled to see a bear with two cubs discover the fish on the trail. That was one happy bear.

Maybe you can guess what happened next. After being up all night, I fell asleep watching the bears.

Screaming woke me. I jumped up and stared out the window. Something large and dark moved in the forested section of the trail. Had a bear been injured? Do bears scream? I didn't know. I clutched my locket. "Daddy, please keep me safe," I whispered.

As I watched, the scene began to make more sense. Not one, but several bears milled about on the trail. Were they fighting over the fish? Had Killer come out of his cabin?

I had to wait until afternoon for my answer. No way was I going to leave the safety of the cabin until all the bears had lumbered back into the woods. With extreme caution, I began moving up the mountain, not on the trail but near it. When I reached the wooded section, I saw what I had both feared and hoped to see—a human leg, some smaller body parts, and a gun. My stomach heaved. "Thanks, Dad," I said to my locket. "I think I'm going to be okay."

I now live in my favorite cabin and have a pretty good vegetable garden going after rescuing vegetable plants and seeds from several other cabins. Every day I stroll down to the dock and visit with Meredith. Every day she invites me to go swimming with her. Do you think I ever so much as dip a toe in that lake water? Ha! I'm not stupid. That is never gonna happen. Some friends you have to keep at arm's length.

The End

Refurbished

You can imagine how annoyed I was when my very loud text notification sound went off at 5:13 in the morning. I leaped out of bed and sprinted down the hall to my home office, wondering what horrific catastrophe could have caused someone to text me at that ungodly hour.

Help me, Bryan.

I didn't recognize the number it came from, and no name popped up, so it had to be some total stranger who texted me by accident and had me mixed up with some other Bryan. Once my heart rate returned to normal, I set the phone down, left it on the charger, and headed back to bed.

The text notification sounded again before I even made it down the hallway. I wanted to ignore it, but what if it wasn't the same person? What if Granddad had taken a turn for the worse? I turned around and trudged back to the phone.

Please help me.

Someone clearly needed help, and thought they were texting someone who could do something about it. I texted back.

I'm sorry, I think you have the wrong number.

95

The answer unnerved me.

No. You're the only one who can help me, Bryan.

I felt bad for this person, but what could I do? I turned off my phone, realizing as I did so that I might as well give up all hope of going back to bed. The phone powered down and then, as I started to lay it back on my desk, it turned itself back on. Instead of the phone company's logo, a photo of a face flashed on the screen: a girl's face, very beautiful, with vivid blue eyes, strawberry blond hair, and a dazzling smile. That's what I get for replacing my old phone with a refurbished one. They must not have wiped all the old data off it.

The image faded instantly, but that didn't make me feel any better. My so-called refurbished phone was acting up the day after I got it. I turned it off again, only to have it turn back on and flash the face again before going to the start screen. Another text popped up.

I'm begging you Bryan. Please help me.

I texted back. *I don't know you. What kind of help do you need?*

Not that I had any intention of taking action, mind you.

To start with, you need to get dressed.

That one creeped me out. How could that other person know if I was dressed or not? Since I couldn't turn the phone off, I muted the sound and left it on my desk while I went to the kitchen to make coffee. If I had no hope of getting more sleep, I might as well make a proper breakfast with eggs and bacon. After work I'd contact my cell provider about the defective phone they'd sent me.

For the first time ever, I wasn't even a little tempted to check my phone at work. In fact, I almost didn't take it with me. I put it in my bottom desk drawer and focused on my work for once. As the day wore on, however, I found it took real effort to not fish out the phone and see if I had any messages.

I had arranged to meet a few friends at a restaurant when I got off, so I had to check and see if anyone had messaged me as soon as I shut down my work computer for the day. My friends hadn't messaged me, but the mysterious stranger had.

Why aren't you answering me, Bryan? Please help me! I need your help!

I gritted my teeth and typed back.

Who are you? Why won't you leave me alone? I'm NOT the Bryan you think I am!

The answer was almost instantaneous.

It's Sarah. I can't leave you alone because I need your help.

So it was a girl! Could there be some connection with the photo that kept coming up on my phone? I couldn't think of anyone I knew named Sarah.

Do you have blue eyes and strawberry blond hair? I sent.

Yes! How did you know?

I didn't answer. Instead I drove to the restaurant and enjoyed a big fat juicy steak with my friends. I told them about the weird messages I had been getting, and my friend Jack had a smart idea.

"You say a photo of the girl keeps appearing on your phone? I bet that phone used to belong to her boyfriend. Most people don't have a picture of themselves as a phone background. And it would make sense if she keeps calling that number. Maybe the boyfriend upgraded and his old phone wasn't completely wiped clean. Either way, you need to contact your phone company."

I knew for a fact I didn't share a phone number with anyone else, but I pulled out my phone right away and texted Sarah.

Do you have a boyfriend?

This time the answer came after a long pause. *Yes.*

What is his name?

Bill. I don't want to talk about him.

I didn't answer. Instead, after eating dessert I said goodbye to my friends and climbed into my car, only to get another text.

Well, if you won't help me, will you at least do me a favor?
What kind of favor? I had to ask.

Go to City Park and pick some flowers for me. Hydrangeas are blooming now, and they're my favorite.

I thought about it. The sun hadn't yet set at 8:00 on a June evening. What would be the harm in driving to the park and picking a few hydrangeas? Nobody would see me. I hoped. Maybe Sarah would shut up and leave me alone if I did it.

Driving to the park, I wondered if I would get to meet Sarah. Why was I picking the city's hydrangeas if not for her? The best hydrangeas did not grow near the still-busy playground, but in a more remote area of the park with green lawns, plenty of wooden benches, and a few huge shade trees. Some amorous couples occupied the benches, but no one looked my way when I picked out a few lovely blue and violet hydrangea blossoms and cut the stems with my trusty Leatherman multitool.

I felt a little silly standing there with my hydrangea bouquet. Clamping the stems under my arm, I pulled out my phone to text Sarah.

What am I supposed to do with these flowers?

Oh! You got them! Thank you! There's a place I want you to put them.

Where? I wanted this game to be over.

You have to go down the walking trail that starts by that vine-covered lamp post.

I knew the trail well, though I hadn't set foot on it in years. The last time, in fact, I had been in sixth grade. As I walked my dog down the trail, a couple of seventh grade bullies stopped me and beat me up. Since then I had avoided the trail, but now it seemed I had no choice. I strolled over there with my flowers, trying to look inconspicuous. At the time, I was so sucked into the whole thing it didn't seem all that weird to be following directions given to me by a girl I'd never met. The clear evening air tasted like wine, and I almost enjoyed my walk down the trail. I walked right past the place where I got beat up and it didn't bother me like I thought it would. Then the next text came in.

When you reach the big rock with moss on it, you have to turn left and leave the path.

Can do, I answered. I saw the rock a few paces ahead, looming on the left side of the trail in the fading daylight.

Step by step, I picked my way forward through the heavy undergrowth, until a new text came in.

Tell me when you get to the clearing with the dogwood tree in it.

I walked for several minutes before I saw anything that could be described as a "clearing," but when I did, it had a dogwood tree in it. I half expected her to be standing there, bathed in the last of the day's light and smiling at me. Instead, I found myself in a small and rather dirty little space, empty of human life except for me. I was more than a little let down.

Do you see the big shrub on the east side of the clearing?

I turned my back to the setting sun and sure enough, I saw a huge shrub with arching branches like a fountain.

Leave the flowers under that shrub, near the trunk.

I was a little creeped out now. Still, I had come this far, so I might as well follow Sarah's nonsensical instructions. Then she'd have to let me off the hook, right? I walked toward the shrub and pulled aside some of the fountain-like branches that sprayed out from the center. Then I tossed my cookies.

Under the shrub lay a long mound of fresh dirt, the exact size and shape you'd expect if someone had recently been buried there. As I stood there, retching, my text notification went off again.

Watch out, Bryan! Bill's there!

How could she know? I whirled around and found myself face to face with a wicked-looking bowie knife. I could only assume the enraged young man on the other end was Bill.

"You stay away from her!" he yelled. "She's mine!"

More than eager to oblige, I kicked Bill in the crotch, threw the hydrangeas at his face, and took off running, not caring that branches caught at my legs and whipped me in the face with every step. I still had my phone in my hand. No way was I going to be this lunatic's next victim. As I ran, I said "Call 911" to my phone and the voice recognition software dialed the number for me. Never have I been a bigger fan of technology than at that moment.

When the dispatcher answered, I kept running and gasped out the details. "In City Park. Found a body! Being chased! He's got a knife!"

By then I had almost made it back to the walking trail. Too bad Bill could run faster than me. Something grabbed my belt from behind and the next thing I knew I was sprawled beside the trail with Bill trying to bring his knife into a useful attack position. I'm a programmer, not a fighter, but that day I fought with everything I had. I kicked. I clawed. I hit. I pulled hair. I'm not sure, but I think I might even have bitten him. I tried and failed to knock the knife out of his hand. He punched and kicked and kept slashing at me with the knife, yelling at me while I yelled back at him. I heard fabric ripping more than once, but didn't know whose clothes had ripped. Had he stabbed through my clothes somewhere? I know at least one time he missed me and drove his knife into the soft ground. It didn't slow him down much. I yelled as loud as I could, hoping someone would hear me, especially someone who wore a policeman's badge. The sun had set and the dusk deepened.

The fight seemed to go on for hours, but in retrospect, I know it couldn't have been more than a couple of minutes. In the midst of the mêlée, I realized I couldn't let Bill get away, even if he stopped attacking me. I had to figure out a way to stay alive and subdue him until help arrived. It's amazing how fast you can think when death seems imminent.

My lucky break came when we rolled toward a patch of ground where several fist-sized rocks lay scattered around. I snatched one up and smashed it down on the hand holding the knife. He dropped the knife, and I wrapped my arms around him and rolled away from it before he could try to grab it again. After that, all I had to do was hold him in a crushing hug while he kept yelling and trying to get away.

My arms were beginning to weaken when the beam of a flashlight hit us. "Break it up, boys," said a voice from behind the light.

Strong arms pulled me away from Bill, and someone else stepped in to grab him.

"I'll kill you!" Bill screamed. "You leave my Sarah alone!" He fought to free himself from the officer's grip, but was no match for the burly policeman.

Within moments, Bill had been handcuffed, and he growled like a wild animal while a gray-haired cop and his big partner held onto him. A policewoman walked up with her dog on its leash. "Where do you think you found a body?"

My breaths came in huge, ragged gasps. "If you give me a minute to catch my breath, I'll show you." I don't like to think what I must have looked like at that moment.

"Son, you belong in the hospital," the older policeman said.

I looked down and saw blood everywhere. On the

ground. On me. On Bill. Whose blood was it? By then a couple of paramedics had joined the party. They helped me to the trail where they had a gurney waiting. The last thing I remember was the older policeman asking Bill, "Is this your bowie knife, son?"

The next time I opened my eyes, I was alone in a hospital room. My left arm, torso, and thigh were bandaged, as I discovered when I took a quick inventory. As far as I could tell, I still had all my body parts. I tried rolling over but thought better of it when pain stabbed through my body. Sleep soon overtook me again, and the next time I awoke, I saw a cop sitting beside my bed, the same old geezer who had rescued me from Bill.

"You're lucky to be alive, son," he said. "You lost a lot of blood."

"I didn't even know I was injured," I admitted.

"You had too many other things on your mind, I guess," he said. "Are you up to answering a few questions? I'm Officer Grimes, by the way."

"Sure."

"How did you find that body? It was nowhere near the trail. Our K9 team found it without trouble, of course, but I would really like to know how you knew to look there."

"I *didn't* know, officer. Someone led me to it."

"And who would that someone be?"

The phone! What happened to my phone? I had dropped it during the fight.

"Is my phone in here somewhere?" I asked. "You're not going to believe me unless I can show you the phone."

"I found a phone at the scene of the fight," he said. "I thought it belonged to your attacker."

"No, that's my phone. I need to show you the texts I got. So weird."

Officer Grimes returned later that day with my phone. I turned it on and as always, the ephemeral image of Sarah flashed on before the home screen came up. I went to the text history so I could show the officer the dozens of texts I'd received, only to find . . . Nothing. There were no texts at all, from Sarah or anyone else. No record of our lengthy text relationship, of her begging and my stalling, of her instructions and my responses. Officer Grimes waited.

"Look," I said, "this is a refurbished phone that I just got, and it's been defective from the get-go. I started getting texts from some girl named Sarah begging me to help her. She told me to pick some flowers and take them to that bush in the forest. Believe me, officer! The texts have all disappeared, but that's how I ended up there. I found a grave under the bush!"

"Yes you did," he said. "The body we found there belongs to a girl named Sarah Reilly. She'd been dead for several days, so how could she have been texting you?"

I felt sick to my stomach. I had no proof at all. I told him the whole story, from the first text till the fight with Bill. At the end, he shook his head. "Son," he said, "that is one wild story, and I wouldn't believe a word of it if the killer hadn't already confessed and if we hadn't found his skin under the girl's fingernails. I just couldn't figure out how you could know about the killing and where to find the body."

"I didn't know she was dead," I said. "Believe me, I didn't know."

A tear trickled down the side of my face. Even if I had

been willing to help her when she first asked, I would have been too late. I didn't even know her, but I hated that she'd died like that, alone and the victim of a violent boyfriend. For some reason, I felt utterly bereft.

Two days after I left the hospital, I saw the announcement in the paper for Sarah's funeral. There had been no new texts from her, and in a way, I kind of missed them. Somehow, in the course of just one day, she had pulled me into her world and now, like it or not, I felt a connection with her that I didn't know what to do about.

I slipped into the back of the chapel. Young people crowded the pews and some older folks too. Sarah's mom wept audibly through the service, and her brother gave a touching tribute to his sister. I wanted to go up to the family and say—I don't know what, but I didn't dare approach them. How could I tell her parents my relationship with their daughter began after she died?

I followed the procession to the cemetery, not because I wanted to, but because I had a mission to complete. Sitting on a gravestone out of earshot, I waited for the graveside service to end and then watched as everyone turned around and trudged back to their cars.

The time had come. The casket still lay up on the surface and the funeral home staff hadn't arrived to lower it yet. As I limped up to the little canopy, I got a text notification. Two words.

Thank you.

I tossed the phone into the hole, underneath the white casket.

"I'm so sorry, Sarah," I said. "You deserved so much better than you got."

Turning away, I hobbled back to my car.

And if you think I'm ever buying another refurbished phone or going near that trail in the park again, you're crazy.

The End

David and Juliette

After David Donovan went to bed that night, I
shut myself in my cabin and forced myself to
open the secret panel that provided access to
the tools of my trade. Sure, I had plenty of specialized
firearms, but I hated using them, and in this instance I knew
I wouldn't. The problem with a gun is that if you use it to kill
someone, everyone knows it's murder. The same holds true
for knives, although I had an impressive collection of them
too—mostly disguised as something else.

No, my go-to weapons were of the more subtle variety.
There was rubio, a rare poison from the Tarantula Nebula.
Tasteless, and it brought on heart failure within minutes,
leaving no trace. The intense red hue posed a problem,
making it unsuitable except for use in drinks or foods that
were already red. I have a fountain pen with another
reservoir in addition to the one containing ink—it contains
the venom of the Threnal scorpion, and the needle which
delivers the venom mimics a scorpion sting. The scorpions
often hitchhike in luggage, which has led to their spread far
beyond the Threnal system, so a sting is almost always
believable.

Another effective device I refer to as the "hairy hat." It

is an attractive and warm hat knitted from a very fuzzy green yarn. However, hidden in the yarn is a network of fibers that interact with the human brain, causing a fatal stroke within fifteen minutes or so. So far I've always been able to retrieve the hat from my victims so I could use it again, hateful as that prospect might be. Have I mentioned I hate my job?

And of course, there were the options specific to my courier ship. I could flood any compartment in the ship with deadly gas—or remove the oxygen. I had only to flip a switch on my pocket controller—but I'd still have to figure out a plausible explanation to give to a board of inquiry, so it was more of a defensive option.

Under normal circumstances, I'd already have completed my assignment by now and be well into the grieving and self-loathing process—but these weren't normal circumstances. Tears streamed down my face as I stared at my weapons. I didn't want to use any of them—not that I ever did, but especially not now. Maybe I imagined it, but the nanobot cluster on my spine seemed to be sending out warning spikes of pain. I ignored them.

My mind went back to how this mission had started. Officially, I'm a courier with the Space Courier Corps of the Universal Business Consortium. Corporations and governments pay me to transport sensitive objects, personnel, or data from one system to another in my high-speed courier vessel, painted in the cheery red and white of the SCC. Courier vessels are immune from attack by pan-galactic agreement, but just in case I still had defensive weaponry both on the inside and outside of my ship.

I received a request from the SCC main office for transport of personnel from Donovan Industries headquarters, one of the largest and most profitable tech companies operating within the Consortium. My heart stopped dead when I saw who they wanted me to carry.

David Donovan, their founder and CEO—and he had requested me specifically. David and I had been in school together—first at the prestigious Apex Academy boarding school, and later in university off-planet. David and I had come to Apex the same year, and our names were close enough alphabetically—David Donovan and Juliette Doyle— that we were always assigned adjoining seats. After just a few weeks, we were good friends.

I know what you're thinking, but you're wrong. We were only thirteen, and there was nothing romantic about our relationship. In fact, I thought of him as a sibling—a very smart and good-looking sibling, but still a sibling. We took many of the same classes and often did our homework together. In tenth grade, we had an assignment in French class to write a summary of an ancient Earth legend, and David was assigned a series of stories about Raynard the crafty fox. Somehow I began calling him Raynard. He retaliated by referring to me as Hermeline, Reynard's foxy wife in the stories. We would leave notes for each other on message boards in the hallways, addressed to "Raynard" or "Hermeline," and written in French. Very few other students studied the obscure language, and the ones that did had no idea who "Raynard" and "Hermeline" were. We were very smug about our little game.

Our senior year of high school, when I faced the prospect of our not ending up at the same university, I began to suspect my feelings for him might be changing into something deeper. I tried to suppress my interest in him. He was from a rich and influential family, and I was a scholarship student from a colony nobody had heard of. His family would never see me as a suitable match for him.

During our years at university, we grew closer and closer. There were many times I could have sworn he was about to express some romantic interest in me—but I always changed the subject. I couldn't bear the thought of

committing to him, only to be rejected by his family. So, like
an idiot, I kept him at arms' length.

When we graduated, his parents gave him an asteroid
with a large manufacturing facility on it. An *asteroid*. I
congratulated him, and I meant it. I had to find work the
old-fashioned way, by applying for it, even though I knew
he would have given me a job if I'd asked for one. My degree
was in biochemistry, but while waiting for a job offer in my
field I took a position with the SCC to pay the bills. I had a
little sister with serious health issues that required
expensive treatment, and I wanted to help. Besides, the
adventure of zipping through space from one system to
another appealed to me. I had plenty of time to read and
keep up with my field while traveling to my various
destinations.

A couple of years into my job as a courier, I went to
visit my parents and my sister Rosemary, as I did whenever I
had time off. She had been looking forward to seeing me for
months, and I breathed a sigh of relief to see that her
condition seemed to have stabilized. My support had made it
possible for my parents to have a full-time caregiver
monitor and care for Rosemary. My last afternoon at home, I
took a walk into the nearby forest for old time's sake, and a
tall imposing man stepped into my path. A large hat, dark
glasses, and a bushy black beard obscured his face.

"We've been watching you," he said. "You're a good
pilot and a discreet courier. I have a business proposal for
you that would quadruple your income."

He wanted me to become a paid assassin. Of course I
said no. Couriers made perfect assassins, he told me,
because we traveled everywhere and were trusted by
everyone. Just think of how well I could treat my family with
this extra income.

"You've got the wrong girl," I said. "I'd never hurt
anyone."

That's when the other shoe dropped. "Oh, accepting our offer is not optional," my recruiter said. "Refusal will lead to immediate execution for you. And your sister Rosemary." He pulled a discreet little disrupter from his vest pocket and pointed it at me to show he meant business. As I gaped at him in shock, he reached out with his free hand and placed it on the back of my neck. I let out a little shriek as I felt a sharp pain like a hornet sting, but much worse.

"That's a little thing we call a compliance guarantee nanobot cluster. By the time this conversation ends, it will have attached itself to your central nervous system. Failure to carry out your assignments will result in excruciating nerve pain. Make a point of defying us and you'll die in agony—and so will your invalid sister."

I've been in the miserable business of killing people for close to eight years now. Every time I've begged to quit, the threat to Rosemary and to me has been renewed and the nanobot cluster has demonstrated just how much pain it could inflict. I've had to go on illegal antidepressants and emotion suppressors just to be able to function and get some relief from the guilt and grief I feel. During that same time, my friend David has built a tech empire worth trillions and is one of the most envied men in the galaxy. We hadn't stayed in touch for more than a year or so after graduation, but I followed his career with interest and often mourned that we hadn't ended up together. Neither of us had married. In my profession, marriage was impossible anyway—and I'd never wanted anyone but David.

Now, he was on my ship and I had to kill him—my best friend and the only man I'd ever loved. We'd had such a great time since he came aboard—talking and laughing about our school days. The moment I saw him, his eyes lit up and he said, "Hermeline!" before giving me a big hug. Tears blurred my vision at the joy of seeing him again and hearing that familiar deep voice. He was so friendly and unassuming —just like always. And more than once we'd locked eyes in a way that made me forget to breathe. I decided to wait until the last possible moment to do what I had to do, and just enjoy every minute that David and I had together. We had another week before we reached the conference location where he would be a keynote speaker. I stopped taking my emotion suppressant soon after he came on board, wanting to fully experience these precious three weeks with him. I also fully experienced guilt, grief, and anxiety.

Two days after my tearful reconnaissance of my weapons locker, David and I enjoyed coffee after dinner in my tiny sitting room with the simulated fireplace. The fake fire crackled and the clock on the mantelpiece chimed softly, harking back to the ambiance of many centuries ago. He had been telling me about the advances his company had made in cloning as a means of providing colony worlds with cheap livestock and protein. Then he stopped talking for a moment and looked at me with those blue, blue eyes. Did I mention his eyes were blue?

"Juliette," he said, "how much are they paying you?"

I shrugged. "Standard courier salary plus a premium bonus for transporting a VIP on this trip."

His gaze didn't waver. "I'm not talking about your official job, Juliette," he said. "How much are you being paid to take me out, and by whom?"

I sat frozen in his gaze. I tried to say something, but words wouldn't come out.

A little half-smile flickered across his face. "You said you've followed my career over the years. Well, I've followed yours too. I have access to sources of information that you probably have never heard of. I've known for years that you are an assassin. I just don't know why. The Juliette I know would never have wanted to kill someone, let alone do it as a profession."

I swallowed hard. "I hate every minute of it," I said at last, "and I've cried over every job they've made me do. I would have quit years ago if it was just my life that would be lost. I've got a compliance nanobot cluster implanted in my spine that will kill me if I fail to carry out an assignment. But they've also got someone in place near Rosemary, and if I fail to eliminate my target, Rosemary will die. I'm trapped and I can't get out."

"Who is 'they?'" he asked.

I shook my head. "I have no idea. They recruited me when I went home on a visit to my family. I think they're some kind of mercenary consortium that people can contact when they want to eliminate someone. I can't prove it, but I think most of us are couriers. We travel everywhere and are immune from attack, so we're the perfect assassins. I'm paid very well to compensate for what I've had to give up. I assume that if I were to get caught, I'd mysteriously die before my trial thanks to the nanobots. And I don't know who's paying my employer to have you eliminated, but they are paying a massive sum."

He nodded. "There are many possible suspects. I requested you as my courier for this occasion, because I knew you'd be assigned to kill me, and I just wanted to see you and have a chance to talk to you. If I understand this correctly, the situation is as follows: you've been hired to kill me. If you succeed, you get a big payoff and I obviously will be dead. If you don't succeed, I survive and your employer kills you and also poor little Rosemary."

"Yes."

"How are you planning to do it?"

Tears streamed from my eyes. "David, I *can't* do it. You're my best friend. I've tried and tried to psych myself up but I just can't. It's been so lovely to see you again and the more time we spend together the more I realize that I can't do it. I'd rather die."

"Come here," he said. He pulled me onto his lap and wrapped his arms around me. "Why didn't you ask me for help? At the beginning or any time since? I've got the resources to get you out of this intolerable situation."

I sobbed on his shoulder. "Why should you help me? I've messed up my life so badly."

"Juliette," he murmured, "I would help you because I love you. There has to be a way out of this."

I took a deep breath. "There is. Until now I've been too cowardly to use it. I've got multiple poisons to choose from. When we arrive at the Macklinburg station, I'll have the autopilot dock the ship so you can exit and then I'll take something before my employer realizes what I've done and activates the nanobots. It will be painless and quick. I wish I didn't have to take Rosemary down with me, but I don't see any way around it."

His grip on me didn't loosen. "One of us has to die," he said. "I don't want it to be you. You're going to have to kill me."

"I already said no. I've made my choice. Besides, no one will care if a courier dies under mysterious circumstances. Whole industries will be disrupted if you die."

He sighed. "So you're saying you won't do it?"

"Yes. I've made up my mind."

"But if I die before we reach Macklinburg, you'll get credit for it, right?"

I pushed away from him and stood up. "What are you saying? You'd kill yourself to keep me alive?"

He stood and put his hands on my shoulders. "You just told me you'd do the same for me. I have my reasons for choosing this fate. Oh, how I wish we could have just picked up where we left off. We could have been so great together, Juliette."

He leaned forward and kissed me. "Now, are you going to give me one of your painless potions, or am I going to have to beg?"

"We've got five more days," I said.

In some ways, those were the happiest five days of my life. At the same time, I found myself obsessing over the situation, trying to figure out a way to work it so that neither of us had to die. No matter how hard I thought about it, I couldn't see a way out. I decided that on that final night before our arrival, I'd take one of my poisons after setting the autopilot to dock my ship, thus forestalling any suicide attempt on David's part. I hoped he would understand. Even more, I hoped there weren't other assassins out there waiting for a chance to eradicate him.

That evening before supper as I sat in my cabin filling out the paperwork on my computer, I received a message from my official employer, the Space Courier Corps. I had a new assignment already. Immediately after delivering David to Macklinburg, I'd been scheduled to transport a pen to his research facility on Charybdis and deliver it to Morna Munro, his director of research. The communication indicated that David would give me the pen, along with further instructions. The pay was even higher than my sky-high bonus for killing David.

Why hadn't he mentioned this? Why would he be willing to pay an astronomical sum for my vessel to transport one little artifact? The original plan had been for me to stay at Macklinburg through the conference and then transport him back to his facility on Scylla, the only other planet in the Charybdis system. Obviously, that was never going to happen. One of us would be dead, and I planned for it to be me.

I stomped out of my cabin and down to the small passenger area. I pounded on David's door. No answer. My heart pounded louder now than my fist had moments earlier. No. Surely not. I turned the door handle, and the door swung open. Just a couple of paces away, David lay on his bed, eyes closed. I ran to him and touched his cheek, to find it already turning cold. My heartbeat thundered in my ears, as if to make up for *his* heart that would never beat again. I kissed his forehead. "No, David, no," I sobbed over and over.

I had cried myself out before I noticed something under his hands, which were neatly folded over his stomach. Wiping tears from my eyes, I pulled out two items. One was a small wooden box, long and thin—about the right size to hold a pen. The other was a note.

My Darling Hermeline/Juliette, it said, *You know I couldn't let you carry out your plan to sacrifice yourself for me. I always carry a potent poison with me in case I am captured by criminals who might want to use my technology for evil purposes, although I would have been happy to use one of yours if you had agreed to it. The last few weeks with you have been so wonderful. I keep asking myself how we somehow didn't end up together after we graduated from university. I have a feeling it is all my fault—I should have pursued you first instead of throwing myself into my business. But that's all water under the bridge. I ask now that you carry out one final little task for me. Take this pen to my research facility on Charybdis and give it to Morna Munro. It has great sentimental value to her and I want her to have it. I've already paid the SCC for the trip. I hope that afterward you will take some time off and remember me fondly. All my love, Reynard/David.*

I grabbed the pen case and opened it, curious to see

what kind of pen could be worth what he had paid to have it transported by itself all the way to Charybdis. I found a fabulous ceremonial pen, engineered to look like an ancient fountain pen. It appeared to be encased in onyx with exquisite platinum tracing. Beautiful, for sure—but what made it so special? I replaced it in the case and returned to my cabin, where I messaged Macklinburg to tell them my VIP passenger had died in his sleep. Without a doubt, there'd be an inquiry. I hoped whatever he took would be untraceable. I didn't want his family to know he had killed himself.

By the time I docked at Macklinburg, my tears had dried and been replaced by numbness. The team from the morgue came and removed David's body and I watched them wheel it away. Dully, I wondered who would speak at the conference in his place. Three hours later, after taking on supplies, I was cleared to leave for Charybdis, a five-week journey at maximum speed.

I spent most of those five weeks in my bunk, curled up into a fetal position and praying for God to end my life. I no longer had the courage to do it myself. A massive deposit showed up in my bank account to reward me for taking out a prime target. The client must have had very deep pockets. I was already a very wealthy woman, but I no longer cared. Over and over, I tried to think what I could have done to stop David from killing himself. I had to reach the conclusion that he made his choice and I couldn't have stopped him, but somehow that didn't comfort me.

When I arrived at Charybdis, a so-called "garden planet," Donovan Industries guards met me and escorted me to the office of Morna Munro. She turned out to be a formidable middle-aged woman, with iron-grey hair, iron-grey eyes, and an ironclad demeanor. So, whatever David's relationship with her had been, it wasn't romantic. I took in a big gulp of air before proffering the pen in its box. "I'm so sorry for your loss," I said. "David was an old friend of mine from school."

She took the box and acknowledged it with a brusque nod. "We've been expecting you, Miss Doyle. Please take a seat in the vestibule until you're called for."

Puzzled, I retreated to the vestibule and sank into one of the comfortable chairs. I completed the assignment, and I had planned to head straight back to my ship. I had more than a month of leave coming and I had permission to take it, in keeping with David's wish as expressed in his final letter.

The minutes dragged by. I found myself becoming more and more drowsy. Had they forgotten about me? Napping would be so unprofessional, but I couldn't keep my eyes open.

I awoke in a darkened room and realized I was lying in a bed—a hospital bed. Was I in a medical facility? What had happened? I didn't feel sick—just tired. I swallowed and ran my tongue over my dry lips. "Hello?"

A skinny young nurse came into the room immediately and turned on a dim light. "How are you feeling, Miss Doyle?"

I sat up. "What's wrong with me? Why am I here? I feel fine. Just a little tired."

He smiled. "I don't know if you realize how very difficult it can be to remove a coercion nanobot cluster, Miss Doyle. The technology is still new and proprietary to Donovan Industries. It took two doctors, dozens of medical nanobots, and six hours to remove and destroy your compliance device."

I stared at him. At the same time I reached my hand to feel the back of my neck—not that I would have felt anything one way or the other. "It's gone?"

He nodded. "Completely removed. You are now free from whomever was controlling you. I'm sorry we had to carry out the procedure without warning you, but you must understand we didn't know what the nanobots might do to you if you guessed what we were planning."

I leaned back against the pillows. Free? I was free? I couldn't even comprehend it. David must have arranged for this before his death. Thinking about David brought tears to my eyes. To have had him for a few weeks, only to have him snatched away forever, broke my heart.

"Where am I?" I asked. "Am I at least still on Charybdis?"

He shook his head. "No, you've been transported to Scylla. Our medical facilities here are better than what's available on Charybdis. Let me bring you some dinner— you've been unconscious for three days."

As I savored the last few bites of my crème brûlée, the nurse came in to retrieve my tray. He carried a neatly-folded stack of my own clothes, and nodded toward a door in the side of the room. "When you've showered and dressed, I'll take you to a much more comfortable room. Take your time. And if you need help, just say so and someone will come right away to assist you."

Half an hour later, I had just finished drying my hair when the nurse returned and motioned for me to follow him. As we walked down a long hallway, I wondered how I would get back to my ship. And what would happen when my shadowy employers realized they no longer controlled me? Would they kill Rosemary?"

We arrived in a room filled with comfortable furniture, which overlooked a lush garden full of greenery and white flowers. A stone fountain splashed in the middle, and I could hear it because the doors and windows were all wide open. I breathed in the heavenly scent of flowers and rain and fertile soil—such a treat for someone who lived in space.

The nurse had left and I stepped forward toward the open door.

"I didn't expect you to actually ignore me," said a voice to my right—a voice I never thought I'd hear again.

Afraid of what I might see, I turned to face the speaker. David, in the flesh, with blue eyes sparkling. I couldn't think of a single thing to say, but once again tears stung my eyes as I witnessed the impossible.

The shadow of a smile flitted across his face. "Think I'm a ghost? I promise you I'm quite solid." He stepped forward and engulfed me in a fierce embrace.

Gasping through my sobs, I finally got a word out. "How?"

"Come sit down," he said, gesturing to a bench in the garden. "You must still be a little weak after your ordeal. You know that one of the many technologies I've pursued is using cloning to provide colony worlds with livestock. Our big breakthrough has been speeding up the process—cloning full-grown animals instead of infants."

I gaped at him, fascinated and repulsed at the same time. "David, you didn't!"

He grinned. "This is why so many people want to kill me. They want to appropriate that technology so they can produce human clone armies or slaves. I can't let that happen, you understand. But I thought it might be in my best interest to have a 'spare' waiting in the wings in case something happened to me."

I didn't know what to think. "You're a clone?"

He shook his head. "No, I'm the real David—your David. The one who died on your ship was a clone. I have a proprietary process for transferring all of my memories and knowledge into a clone. That David you transported was 'me' in almost every way. He had my memories, knew our history together, and knew what his mission was. He knew you had been contracted to kill me, and because he basically *was* me, he loved you and was willing to sacrifice himself for you if necessary."

"What was the pen for, then?"

"The pen served two purposes. First, I had to get you here so that my staff could remove your compliance nanobots. It's a very dicey business and I didn't trust anyone else to do it. Secondly, I needed you to bring me the memories of the clone, preserved in a memory device inside the pen. He downloaded them to the pen before taking his life, and I needed those memories to know how the trip had gone and whether I had any hope of a future with you."

My head reeled until I felt lightheaded. "But what about Rosemary?"

"I suggest that your courier ship might have a catastrophic accident shortly after leaving Charybdis. You will be declared dead and your family will inherit your very healthy bank balance. Perhaps in a few years you could even pay them a secret visit."

I stood and paced on the garden path in front of him. "But everyone thinks you're dead! How will you explain what's happened?"

"I won't, Juliette. Let them think I'm dead. I have a massive estate here on Scylla, and everyone here thinks I'm a former Donovan Industries executive named David Reynard. When they tell me I look like myself, I say I'm flattered. Morna's the only one who knows who I really am."

I giggled. "Reynard? Really? The fox?"

He grinned. "It seemed appropriate. What I'm trying to say is that I have plenty of resources to start over. I've been planning it for a while. You and I—we could start our own biochemistry lab and work together as husband and wife. Change the world—or the universe."

I batted my eyelashes at him. "Why, Mr. Reynard, is

that a proposal?"

He stood and pulled me close. "Is this an acceptance, Miss Hermeline?"

I put my arms around his neck and smiled into those blue eyes.

Together, we both said "Yes."

The End

Dream

E ven with the window open and my bed right beside it, I lay drenched in perspiration, unable to sleep. Our dorm's air conditioning had gone out not in the early spring, when it wouldn't have mattered, but at the end of May when the school year was almost over and the weather was hot. I looked out the window at the hospital across the street. I bet they had air conditioning. Begging the universe at large for the release of slumber, I hoped I wouldn't dream of being in a sweltering jungle.

As it turned out, my very vivid dream didn't involve a jungle at all. I found myself in a forest on a mountainside, which had patches of snow on the ground. Fresh cold air blew on my face, but the rest of me remained warm. I looked down and saw I wore warm leather boots laced up over thick woolen trousers of some kind, and a fleece-lined leather coat. Putting my bare hands in the pockets of my coat, I walked forward on the path which lay ahead of me.

Within a few minutes, I came to a clearing with a neat cottage on the other side of it. Some part of me knew it was a dream, and I thought it was a pretty boring one so far, so I turned aside and approached the cottage.

A teenage girl came around from behind the cottage,

with two large buckets in her hands. She dropped them and ran forward to greet me. Her first words? "Are you the dark prince?"

"Uh, no," I said. "I'm just a college student. My name is Spencer Paul."

"My mother has the second sight," the girl said, as if that somehow explained the situation. "She has foreseen that Pearlie will be rescued by a dark prince. Wait here while I go get her. She'll know who you are."

More mystified than ever, I stood in the middle of the clearing wondering what to do. I pulled my right hand from my pocket and inspected it. How dark did it have to be? My skin is a rich chocolate brown, thanks to my Kenyan mother.

In a few moments the girl returned with an older version of herself, a tall, dignified woman with piercing dark eyes.

"Aha," she said. "You've come at last, then."

"I don't know what's going on," I said, "but I'm not who you think I am. I'm just a student—not a prince."

"You can be a prince and not know it," the woman said. "Approach me, my son. I must be sure."

"She won't hurt you," the girl assured me.

I stepped forward and the woman put her hands on either side of my face and stared deeply into my eyes, a process that was more than a little unnerving for an introvert like myself. I felt somehow as if my soul, my whole inner landscape, was laid bare in the beam of that gaze.

Taking a deep breath, she released me. "Yes," she said. "It is you and no other. For two years we have awaited your coming. Jillian will take you to Pearl—but I warn you, you must be on your guard every moment. The dragon comes and goes at unpredictable times."

From a dream standpoint, that sounded promising. Jillian wrapped herself in a heavy woolen cloak and motioned for me to follow her. Our path took us up the mountain. After only thirty minutes of climbing we had come out above the treeline. Another ten minutes of us climbing and me panting for breath found us on a snow-covered rocky ledge that would have been large enough to park several school buses.

Jillian pointed to the side of the mountain on the far side of the ledge. "If you can see that dark spot—that's the cave where Pearlie is held prisoner. I am bound by the dragon to serve her and take care of her physical needs. If I refuse, my parents will be incinerated."

"I still think you've got the wrong guy," I said. "I've never heard of anyone named Pearlie and I know nothing about dragons."

"Mother is never wrong," Jillian said. "Please wait a moment while I make sure it's safe. Sit down behind this rock. I am not in danger since it's my job to be here."

She began to pick her way across the ledge, following a path that had clearly been used many times. The snow was packed down and covered with footprints. Soon she returned, smiling. "All clear," she said. "Just be sure to keep on the path so your footprints won't be so obvious."

I followed her across the snow to the cave. Larger than I had expected, the opening was maybe twenty feet across and ten feet high. No door or fence blocked it from the bitter wind, but I could see some kind of wooden structure inside. A door in the structure opened and a girl emerged. Tall and slender, she had hair like burnished copper and golden-brown eyes. She shot a questioning look at Jillian.

"The dark prince," Jillian said. "He's come at last."

Pearl nodded. "Thank you so much for coming."

"Look," I said. "There's been a terrible mix-up. I'm just a student. I don't even know what it is you want me to do. Why can't you just walk out of the cave and come back to Jillian's cottage with us?"

"We'll have to show him," Jillian said. "And then run for our lives." Motioning me to stay put, she stepped forward and crossed into the cave. Once inside, she pulled a wrapped package from her cloak and handed it to Pearl. "Your supper," she said.

Then she stepped back out, across the imaginary line which denoted the entrance to the cave.

Pearl watched without comment. "Get ready to run as fast as you can," Jillian warned.

I tensed my tired muscles, wondering what on earth to expect. Pearl stepped toward me, her eyes wide with fear. The moment her toe touched the unseen line of demarcation, the entire opening of the cave became a roaring sheet of flame, as if a bomb had gone off. Pearl leapt backward. Jillian grabbed my hand and yelled, "Run!"

I ran. I wasn't sure what I was running from, but I didn't want to stick around to find out. Just as Jillian and I reached the cover of the forest, an outraged scream split the air. Jillian pulled me down behind a snow-covered fallen tree trunk.

We watched as an enormous red dragon blotted out the sky on its way to the cave. A huge tongue of flame shot from its mouth and nostrils as it flew.

"I can come and go as I please," Jillian whispered, "but if Pearlie so much as touches the line across the entrance to the cave, the fire barrier goes up and Queen Ann somehow knows it. It's like an alarm of some sort in addition to being a barrier. And the queen always comes to investigate. The same thing would happen if you or anyone else were to try and walk *into* the cave."

The dragon landed on the ledge but we couldn't see what happened after that. According to Jillian, the dragon was most likely treating Pearl to some kind of verbal abuse. We stayed where we were until we saw the huge red beast fly away from the mountain.

I followed Jillian back down to the cottage. "I am so confused," I said. "Where does the queen come into this? And what's her relationship with the dragon?"

"They're the same person," Jillian said. "The queen of Doloria is a shape-shifter. I have seen her human form, but Pearlie never has. She always comes to Pearlie as a fire-breathing dragon."

"What on earth did Pearl do to offend her?" I asked.

Jillian opened her mouth to reply, but I never heard her answer. I woke up in my dorm room, soaked in sweat, and bathed in the light of the morning sun.

"Must have been some dream," my roommate commented. "You were apparently trying to run."

I sat up and saw my bedding in a heap on the floor.

"The dream ended too soon," I said.

Have you ever wanted to go back to a dream somehow? That was me all day that day as I went to classes and studied for exams. That night when I lay down by the window again, I could think of nothing but Pearl and Jillian. Not that I believed the "dark prince" stuff, but I did at least want to know what Pearl had done to merit such severe treatment.

I know it seems unlikely, but as soon as I closed my eyes, I found myself back in Doloria. Not in the cottage where Jillian's family lived, but on the icy ledge in front of Pearl's cave. In fact I had appeared only ten feet or so from that dangerous barrier. It must have been early morning, for the cave and the entire ledge were in deep shadow as the bulk of the mountain hid the rising sun. I looked around for any sign of the red dragon and was greeted by an empty, silent sky.

"Pearl!" I called hoarsely, trying not to make too much noise but wanting her to hear me. I called a couple more times before the wooden door inside the cave opened and Pearl's face appeared, holding her finger to her lips. She withdrew again, but soon reappeared wrapped in blankets and came to face me, well within her boundary.

"Why have you come so early in the morning? What is your plan?" she demanded. "And what is your name?"

The only question I could answer was the last one, so I said, "My name is Spencer Paul."

She giggled. "You have two first names. Or two last names."

I grinned at her. "Yeah. I'm used to it. I have to ask you though, what did you do to merit this treatment? Are you a criminal?"

This time she laughed out loud. "Didn't Jillian tell you? I was never told what my offense was. I woke up from a deep sleep and I was here, in the cavern, and Queen Ann in her dragon form was looming over me. She said, 'Don't think you can escape me so easily, young lady. You will be my prisoner here until you die or I choose to release you.'"

"Does your family know what's happened to you?" I asked.

At this her expression changed to one of sorrow. "I have trouble remembering my family," she said. "Jillian thinks the queen put some kind of spell on my memory. I have sort of a vague impression that my mother was very cruel to me and my father was kind, but every time I try to remember details they slip away from me. And it doesn't help that the dragon is always asking me questions about them and it just makes me anxious. It seems sometimes like she's trying to make me crazy. Maybe I already am."

"I want to help you," I said, "but I don't know how."

In the back of my mind I kept reminding myself that this was a dream and nothing too terrible could happen to me.

"The dragon has told me over and over that nothing can destroy the barrier she has put in place here," Pearl said. "Jillian's mother Jacqueline told me the only way to break this particular kind of enchantment is to kill its originator. If the dragon dies, all her enchantments die with her."

I did not like the sound of this. Did they expect me to slay this dragon that was the size of a house? "I've never killed anything," I said. "Not even a mouse. How on earth do you expect me to defeat a dragon?"

Pearl shook her head. "I don't know. All I know is that you're the one to do it. And you should probably get some white clothes if you're going to keep coming here, so you'll blend in better with the snow." Suddenly fear transformed her face. "She's coming! You've got to hide somehow or she'll kill you!"

A large snowdrift had accumulated against the side of the mountain on each side of the cave. I ran to the left and dove into the snow, turning around to face outward and pulling more snow down over me until only a tiny opening was left, through which I could see and breathe. If Pearl had already seen the dragon, there's no way I would have had time to reach the trees.

The massive dragon circled for a few moments before skidding to a halt in front of the cave. To my relief, her landing wiped out any tracks I might have made.

"Pearl!" said the dragon. To my surprise, she had a very melodious and almost seductive voice.

A few moments elapsed before I heard Pearl's voice, which sounded plausibly sleepy. "What do you want, your majesty?"

"Oh, you know me. I just like to keep you on your toes. Maybe you're more likely to remember when you first wake up. What is your last name again?"

Pearl said nothing.

"Is that too hard for you? What about your mother's name? Your father's name?"

Pearl remained silent.

"You're so pathetic," the dragon said. "Don't know anything, can't remember anything, can't do anything but feel sorry for yourself. And don't think I haven't heard that absurd prophecy about the dark prince. If there were a dark prince in my kingdom I would know and would already have killed him. Like this."

The dragon blasted a stream of flame at a boulder that sat on the ledge about fifty feet from me. The snow on the boulder melted, the boulder itself began to glow, and then it cracked into many pieces, which sizzled as they fell into the snow.

The dragon continued to verbally abuse Pearl in her sickly-sweet voice until the poor girl sobbed loudly enough for me to hear. By then I was in trouble myself, soaking wet from the snow and beginning to lose feeling in my hands and feet. The dragon finished her tirade and then swirled around to face outward for takeoff. Her tail dug into my snowdrift and exposed my leg, but she did not turn around before spreading her wings and leaping from the ledge.

As soon as that red monster was out of sight, I shook off as much wet snow as I could and ran forward to talk to Pearl, but she had already turned her back. She ran into her wooden box and slammed the door.

This time I was on my way down to Jillian's house when I woke up.

For the remaining twelve days of the semester, I spent every night dreaming of Doloria and Pearl. I now called her Pearlie too. Smart, resourceful, and compassionate, she drew me into her world and I found myself growing closer and closer to her. I knew I was in trouble, falling for a girl who didn't exist except in my dreams. And despite having spent hours talking to Pearlie and Jillian and her parents, I was no closer to coming up with a plan to defeat the all-powerful dragon. If only I could somehow have a gun in my dream—but I couldn't.

I wrote my last exam, loaded my belongings into my vintage Volkswagen Beetle, and drove the forty-five minutes to the family home on the outskirts of town. My parents have sixteen acres, an orchard, and a huge vegetable garden. As I drove down the road to our house, something bright kept flashing in my eyes. Mystified, I pulled up in front of the house to see my dad in the yard with a rather large cardboard contraption that was very bright silver on one side.

I climbed out of the car and walked over to hug him. "What the heck is that, Dad?"

"It's a solar cooker design I'm working on," he said. "Remember the last time we went to Kenya to visit your mother's family? She was concerned about the deforestation and the lack of firewood for people to cook with. She wants me to come up with an affordable solar cooker that we can show people over there how to make."

His apparatus was large—close to four feet in diameter —but it was made of cardboard. The wedge-shaped panels were coated in bright silver plastic of some kind and formed into a bowl shape. A metal pipe stuck out from the middle of the bowl and supported a metal ring. Dad showed me how to orient the device to focus the sun's rays so they bounced back and joined together at the focal point—the metal ring. We put a thin aluminum pot of water on the ring and timed it—twenty-seven minutes to boil two quarts of water.

"Jeddy!" yelled my dad. "Come out and see this!" My mother came out to see the water boil and then used it to make tea—after giving me a big hug and congratulating Dad on the success of his experiment.

An idea began to form in my head. I was an engineering student myself. I understood about parabolas and focal points. What if I could somehow turn the dragon's breath back using a dish with a focal point of about forty feet? All that fire would converge and focus, and my job would be to aim it at the dragon's head from forty feet away. It sounded crazy, but it was the closest thing to a plan I'd had yet. And after all, it was only a dream.

I worried I might not return to Doloria that night. After all, I wasn't in my dorm at school anymore. What if that world was lost to me forever? My concern made it harder for me to fall asleep, but when I did I found myself back in Doloria, this time in Jillian's cottage.

"I hate how you just appear and disappear," Jillian said. "But anyway, at least you're here. We've made you some white clothes that can go over your other clothes." She and her mother had already painted my boots white with some herbal substance they had.

"Thank you so much. In fact it's perfect because I've had an idea," I said, "but I'll need help to carry it out."

"What kind of help?"

I thought. In this medieval society, who could help me? "I think I need a blacksmith."

Jacqueline, who had been quietly knitting in the corner, nodded. "Better take him down to the village to see Glenn. May I ask what you're after?"

"Well, I guess first I need a large round metal shield. Then I'll need a blacksmith to modify it for me."

"Shields are useless if you're up against a dragon," said Jacqueline's husband Stephen. "Even if you somehow escape the flames, the shield would heat up until it was red hot and you'd be terribly burned by the metal."

"This shield will be like no shield you've ever seen," I said. "But I have no money for a shield." How did one pay for things in Doloria? I had no idea.

Stephen and Jacqueline exchanged a meaningful glance, and then he climbed up into the loft of the cottage. He soon returned with two items: a very dusty metal shield and an old sword in its scabbard. "These belonged to my father," he said, "many years ago. As a woodsman I have no need of them. If they can help you in your fight against the dragon, you are welcome to them."

"I won't need the sword," I said. "But the shield is a

good start. You say you know a blacksmith in the village? How can I earn enough to pay him?"

"Tell him why you need the work done and see what he says," Stephen said. "Whatever price he names, tell him you'll pay it. If necessary, we'll take up a collection from everyone in the village. Every person in this community would love to see the dragon's power broken. And by now they all know you are the dark prince who can do it."

I still hated the "dark prince" talk. But I was more and more motivated by my compassion and affection for Pearlie. Two years she'd suffered!

Jillian led me farther down the mountain to the nearest village, a location I had not yet visited in Doloria. It was easy to find the blacksmith by the smoke and the sound of hammer striking anvil. I carried the large round shield on a strap over my shoulder.

"Glenn," Jillian said, "no doubt you've heard of our friend Spencer, the dark prince. He has at last devised a plan he thinks might defeat the dragon, but he needs your help."

Glenn the blacksmith put down his hammer and removed his leather gloves. "You have my full support, young man," he said. "Tell me your plan, and if it seems reasonable to me, I will work for free. I have spent the last two years trying to think of a way to free that poor girl."

I balanced the shield on top of two sawhorses. "I need you to take off the grip and arm guard. Then the shield will need to be made into a very specific shape, which I should be able to show you the next time I come. Then the concave side will need to be polished to a very bright shine, and I will need two hand grips on the convex side."

"You want a backwards shield?" Glenn said, his bafflement obvious.

I nodded. "If we get the curve right, the focal point will be about forty feet away. Which is the closest I ever want to get to that dragon."

He shrugged. "I don't even know what a focal point is."

I was in the middle of explaining it when I woke up in my bedroom at home. I didn't mind not getting to see Pearlie during the night's dream, because now I had a plan to help her. I spent an hour working out in my parents' home gym. I realized it was kind of ridiculous—working on my real, physical muscles when it was the dream me who needed strength—but I did it anyway.

My next task was to sit down at my dad's big desk and work out the parabolic curve I'd need the shield to have. I'd have to memorize it, because obviously I couldn't trace it onto a sheet of paper and take it with me.

My final project of the day was a little trickier from the standpoint of having to explain myself to my parents. I taped a piece of paper to the outside back wall of the garage. Then, using my dad's metal tape measure, I placed a series of orange tent stakes in the grass exactly forty feet from my paper target. They formed a nice semicircle.

My parents seemed a little amused by all the activity. They had expected me to spend the first few days of summer vacation lounging on the couch in front of the television or going to the lake with my sister, who was home from grad school for the summer, and who found all my activity irritating. "Sit down for a minute," she said. "It makes me tired just watching you."

I ignored her and went back outside to my tent stakes. My goal was to become so familiar with what forty feet looked like from any angle that I'd be able to focus my parabolic shield with relative ease.

All the activity of the day ensured a good night's sleep that night. I had no control over where I appeared in Doloria, and tonight I was glad to find myself on the ledge by Pearlie's cave.

Pearlie sat huddled a few feet back from her boundary, sobbing. I checked the sky and saw the dragon in the distance, flying away from the mountain.

I stepped as close to the barrier as I dared. "Was she just here? What did she say to you?"

She lifted her head to look at me and I saw something in her face I hadn't seen before—despair. "I'm never getting out of here," she said. "The dragon has been saying that all along and I realize she's right. I know you want to help me, and I appreciate it, but what can you do? The queen is too powerful. She would fry you to a crisp before you got anywhere near close enough to attack her."

I knelt down so I could look directly at her. "Listen to me, Pearlie. Things have changed. I have an idea—a plan. It's going to take a few days to get everything ready, but you can't give up yet! Remember I'm really new at this dark prince business. I'm trying to learn on the job."

That earned me a smile. "I like your new white clothes."

"They're just my regular pants and jacket with white coverings," I admitted, "but they'll be perfect for my plan."

"Can you tell me your plan?"

By now I had heard the dragon verbally abusing and questioning Pearlie on three separate occasions. If she didn't know anything, she couldn't reveal anything.

"No, I'm sorry. If you knew the plan the dragon might somehow force you to reveal it," I said.

She nodded. "You're right. Don't tell me anything!"

I stayed with her, trying to comfort and cheer her, until Jillian arrived with food and water.

"Ah," she said when she saw me. "You'd better come all the way down to the village with me. Glenn needs more instructions."

Pearlie perked up at that tiny piece of information. I just winked at her before turning to follow Jillian.

In the village, Glenn showed me what he'd done to the shield so far. The attachments on the concave side had been removed and the surface ground down, but it was a long way from being shiny.

"I don't know what kind of handles you want," he said.

"First things first," I said. "I need a big piece of paper or a flat board and a measuring stick of some kind. And something to write with."

When these items had been procured, I reproduced my calculations from memory and drew the radius of the parabola on the piece of parchment, explaining to Glenn that the shield would have to match this curve.

He nodded. "I will have to hammer the shield out to make it thinner and wider," he said. "Not my favorite job, but I can do it."

"Once the curve is perfect, the concave surface will need to be polished like a mirror," I continued.

He shook his head. "I can make it shiny, but if you want a mirror shine, we will need to plate it with silver. Steel simply isn't bright enough."

Jillian, who had been watching and listening, spoke up. "I'll go around the village and tell everyone to spread the word that you need silver and that it is for defeating the queen."

After she left on her errand, Glenn looked at me. "So many of our hopes depend on you, young man. Pearlie may be the only actual prisoner, but the rest of us are slaves to the queen's whims also. I hope you know what you're doing."

I hoped that too. But in the back of my head, all the time, was a tiny voice saying, "It's a dream. Even if you fail and the dragon incinerates you, you'll still wake up safe in your own bed." I hated that voice. What would happen to Pearlie if I failed?

Over the next few days and nights, I poured myself into

my preparations. I wondered if I was actually getting enough rest, what with all the activity in my dreams. When awake, I focused on working out and learning to judge a forty-foot distance from any angle. In Doloria, I alternated between trying to keep Pearlie's spirits up and working with Glenn on my shield. When I explained to him how it would work, he was very helpful in designing handles that wouldn't absorb the heat from the shield—at least not right away. The village saddler wrapped the handle grips with several layers of thick leather to further insulate them.

While Glenn and I worked on the shield, the villagers and residents of the surrounding area had been bringing a steady stream of silver trinkets and jewelry until Glenn declared he had enough. The shield was huge—five feet in diameter, but quite thin. It took real strength to lift it and I practiced whenever Glen wasn't actively working on it. Secretly, I hoped when the time came I'd be able to rest the shield on the ground and still aim it with accuracy.

When I showed up to find the shield silver plated and shining every bit as bright as my dad's solar cooker, my stomach did a few flip-flops. There was no going back now. The back of the shield had already been painted white. Now I asked Jacqueline to make a white cloth cover for the front of the shield—something that would burn away instantly when the dragon attacked. I just didn't want to advertise my presence before I was ready.

"Are you sure you don't need a sword?" Glenn asked.

"I'd be dead long before I could get close enough to use a sword," I said.

"I'm afraid you'll be dead one way or the other," he said, "but I hope I'm wrong. I will see that the shield is transported up to Jillian's cottage so you won't have to haul it all the way up the mountain yourself. You need to conserve your strength."

The next evening at home I felt restless and out of

sorts. The last several weeks had all led up to this: a nerdy engineering student believing that somehow he could rescue an imaginary dream girl from an imaginary dream dragon. I stayed up late visiting with my parents and my sister before going to bed.

This time I appeared on the ledge. It was dark, except for moonlight, but whether evening or morning, I couldn't tell. To my surprise, I saw the shield propped up in a snowdrift beside the cave. Part of me hated that Jillian had risked bringing it up here where it might be detected—but the rest of me was glad I didn't have to haul it up from the cottage.

I assumed Pearlie must be sleeping, and it struck me this was ideal. I could set off the alarm, the dragon would come, and maybe it would all be over by the time Pearlie woke up. I had no reason to wait—unless cowardice counts as a reason.

I stepped up to the cave entrance and moved my foot right up to the boundary line. Flames shot up all across the barrier, and in my hurry to escape I fell down and had to roll away in a most undignified manner. I scrambled over to the shield and crouched down behind it, holding the handles with the spare pair of leather blacksmith's gauntlets Glenn had loaned me.

Mere minutes later, I heard the dragon's squeals of rage. Flames lit the night sky as she approached. She came in fast and almost slid over the still-flaming barrier.

"You should know better than that, Pearl," she said. That was my cue.

"Pearl does know better than that," I said, staying where I was but standing up to look over the rim of the shield. The dragon turned her head and her long neck to look at me.

"I suppose you think you're the dark prince," she said.

"My identity is unimportant," I answered, firming my grip on the handles.

"You're right," she replied, "seeing as you'll be burnt to a crisp a few seconds from now." She drew her head up and back in preparation for striking. "Your pathetic wooden shield will only delay your death by a second or two."

She took a deep breath and then blasted a stream of flame at me. I stepped forward to meet it, knowing I wasn't quite at the forty-foot mark.

The fire burned away the cloth covering instantly, and the mirrored surface of the shield deflected the flames. In the darkness, it was easy to orient the shield so the focal point was the dragon's head. It takes much longer to tell about than it did to happen. The flame struck the shield; the shield reflected the flames, I aimed the focal point at the dragon's head, the dragon's head exploded with a tremendous BANG; and I dropped the red-hot shield into the snow.

The dragon's body fell to the ground with a loud thud that seemed to shake the mountainside. My first thought was, it's not murder if you kill an imaginary beast. . . .

"Spencer?"

I looked up to see Pearlie standing in the entrance of the cave, staring at the body of the dead dragon. This was the moment of truth. If Jaqueline was right, the spell should be broken. I strode toward Pearlie and kept going when I reached that hated line. Nothing happened. I walked into the cave, put my arms around Pearlie, and hugged her like I'd never hugged anyone before.

"Come on," I said. "You've got your whole life ahead of you."

She smiled up at me and held my hand as we both walked out of the cave and headed across the ledge toward the path. Then I woke up in my dark bedroom at home.

Roaring in frustration, I looked at the clock beside my bed and it was only 3:00 in the morning. Why had I woken up so early? Why did I have to leave Pearlie when I finally rescued her? It was over an hour before I fell asleep again, and it was a deep, dreamless sleep such as I hadn't had in over a month.

A couple of hours later, I stumbled into the kitchen feeling grumpy and cheated. Dad was brewing coffee to take in a thermos to work with him, while munching on some eggs and sausages. "Ready for your workout?" he asked.

I growled in response. Dad flipped on the morning news like he always did while eating his breakfast.

"A local girl has woken up from a coma after two years," the anchorman intoned. A photo flashed onto the screen and I almost fell off my chair. It was Pearlie—maybe a little bit younger, but definitely her. "Eighteen-year-old Pearl Baker has been in an unexplained coma for two years," the anchorman elaborated. "Early this morning she woke up and although doctors say she is disoriented, she otherwise seems healthy. Unfortunately her mother won't hear the good news, because in a tragic coincidence, Ann Baker died in a car accident at about the same time as her daughter recovered."

I stared at the screen, slack jawed. What did it mean? If Pearl was real, I had to go see her. And if her mother's name was Ann...

After Dad left for work, I showered and put on what I hoped was an attractive outfit. I looked up the news online and found out which hospital Pearl was in: the one right across the street from my university dorm. "Going into town for a while," I told Mom.

I stopped to buy some white roses because I thought Pearlie would like them. It wasn't until I stepped onto the elevator that would take me to her floor in the hospital that I had second thoughts. What was I doing? Barging in on a poor girl who'd been in a coma for two years? Just because she looked like the girl in my dreams? And had the same name?

I took a deep breath as I stepped off the elevator. Sooner than I was ready, I found room 435. I knocked.

"Come in," said a voice. A voice I recognized.

I stepped into the room with my bouquet of roses, focusing on the girl in the bed, who sat brushing her long copper-colored hair. Her eyes sought mine and her face lit up with delight. "Spencer! You're real!"

Relief flooded my body. "Hi Pearlie," I said, grinning so widely my face hurt. I held out the flowers and she took them and inhaled their aroma before setting them down on her bedside table and indicating that I should sit on the end of the bed.

"You really did save me," she said. "Somehow, I think that dragon was my mother. My parents are divorced and I was forced to live with my criminally insane mother. She was so abusive that I think I must have fallen into a coma to escape her. But she followed me to Doloria and kept me a prisoner there too. That's why I couldn't wake up from the coma—until you came."

I wondered if she knew what had happened to her mother. "I heard your mother was in an accident," I said.

She grimaced. "They told me she was driving here to the hospital when her car basically blew up. Burst into flames."

We stared at each other. I was thinking maybe I hadn't been as safe from harm in my dream as I believed myself to be. And did her mother's death make me a murderer? Another thought struck me. I stared out of Pearlie's window —directly across the street and into my recently-vacated dorm room. Had she somehow reached out to me while in her coma?

The door to the room burst open and a man strode in. We both turned to look at him and I found myself surprised once again, this time to see Glenn, the blacksmith from Doloria. "Pearl! Baby!" he said. "Thank God you're all right.

I came as quickly as I could." He leaned over the bed and gave her a big hug.

"Daddy!" she said. "Oh, Daddy, it was awful! Can I please live with you now?"

"I absolutely insist," he said. Then he turned to me and held out his hand to shake mine. I ignored it and stood to give him a big hug, which he returned. After what we'd been through together, a handshake seemed so inadequate.

"Spencer," he said. "I see you and Pearl have already found each other. In Doloria I didn't know who she was, except that I loved her and wanted her to be free. Thank you so much for everything you did. You gave my daughter back to me. It's a miracle she has survived her mother's psychological abuse—both here and in Doloria."

"I couldn't have done it without your help," I said.

Glenn beamed at me and then at Pearlie. "Let's hope none of us ever sees Doloria again."

I was fine with never seeing Doloria again—but I had every intention of seeing as much as possible of Pearlie.

The End

Handshake

Please understand, I've always stayed on the right side of the law. I've never used my gift to do anything illegal. Which is why I feel maybe I need to explain what I'm doing in jail.

When I was a tiny tot of five, my parents took me on a trip to Ireland so we could all see where our ancestors came from. Like I cared. But anyway, we stayed with some distant cousin in County Clare, and I was let loose in the garden to play so the grownups could talk. My ball rolled under some shrubs, and as I crawled in on hands and knees to get it, I saw something moving in the leaf litter.

Thinking it might be a bunny rabbit, I pounced and grabbed it with my hand. It wasn't a bunny rabbit. It was a tiny little man wearing green clothes, and he was infuriated. He yelled at me in his high little voice, but I hung onto him because I couldn't help it. What little girl wouldn't want a living toy?

"Don't think I'm going to tell you where my gold is, Riley Quinn!" he shrieked.

At that age, what was gold to me? "I don't want it," I said. "I just want to keep you."

"Well, that's right out," he huffed in his thick Irish

brogue. "How about some magic? Would you like some magic?"

Wouldn't you? I held him up right in front of my face and nodded.

I don't know what I expected. Maybe to be transformed into a dazzling princess, like Cinderella. He closed his eyes, muttered a string of gibberish, and then my right hand, which still held him tight, was apparently hit by invisible lightning that stung like needles. Startled, I dropped my tiny captive, who promptly disappeared. My hand still tingled and in the dim light under the bush, it glowed a little.

By the time I grabbed my ball and crawled back out onto the lawn to show my parents my cool glowing hand, the glow had faded and my right hand looked just like my left hand. I felt gypped.

It took several months of chance occurrences and experimentation for me to realize that my right hand really *was* magic. If I touched someone else's right hand, and then asked for something, they *always* gave it to me. I soon learned to grab my mother's right hand and hang onto it before asking for a snack or a new toy.

By the time I was a teenager I began to comprehend the magnitude of my special gift. Guess who got a brand-new red Camaro for her sixteenth birthday? Guess who dated the hunkiest football player? I went to college and majored in business, figuring that as a business person I'd be doing a lot of handshaking, which could only guarantee my success. Every conference with one of my professors ended with me getting my grade raised—though to be fair, I mostly earned my 4.0 average.

I tried a few different businesses before getting into real estate back in my home state of Louisiana. I tried not to be greedy. . . well, at least most of the time. I'd see a "for sale" sign in front of a house, walk up to meet the owners, and after an innocent handshake I found they could be happy with a much lower price than they had originally asked for. Contractors gave me great deals on the labor to fix the houses up, and then when I put the properties back on the market, prospective buyers who shook my hand suddenly discovered they were willing to pay a higher price than they'd planned.

I socked away my earnings in various bank accounts, living for the day when I'd have enough to live on without having to work at all—just fix up a fabulous historic mansion in an out-of-the way place where I would surround myself with pretty things, a place that would be my refuge when I wasn't traveling. My goal was almost in reach when I met old Mrs. Lambert in the check-out line at the grocery store in Alexandria, Louisiana. I had settled there for the time being, as it was close to where I'd grown up. She seemed a little confused and anxious. Because I am a nice person, I helped her figure out where her wallet was and then find the right amount of cash. She was so grateful.

As I was only buying a couple of items myself, I offered to help her get her things out to her car. Her car turned out to be a sleek predatory-looking silver Jaguar. I have to admit, my curiosity was piqued. This is not your typical old-lady kind of car, and she hadn't struck me as being in the sort of income bracket that could pay for a luxury car. I helped her load her things into the trunk and then tried to keep the conversation going. She mentioned being lonely, and I had my opening. I shook her hand in parting, saying, "You know, I'm lonely too, Mrs. Lambert. I grew up in this area, but it seems so different since I moved back a few months ago. Maybe I could meet you for a cup of coffee sometime."

Instantly she invited me to come over for coffee the very next afternoon. I had to pull out my little notebook to write down the detailed directions to her house, which was out in the country. I swear, at that moment I was motivated only by idle curiosity and a genuine fondness for the sweet old lady.

Other motivations might have come into play when I rolled up to the entrance of her place and gaped at the gigantic elaborate wrought-iron gates, which had been left open, giving them a hospitable look. The house didn't come into view until I'd driven a couple hundred yards down the crape-myrtle-lined driveway, which was covered with the pink and white confetti of the fallen blossoms. Classic old Louisiana mansion with the pillars and verandas and the huge live oaks surrounding the immaculate green lawn. The moment I saw it, I wanted to live there for the rest of my life —but I already liked Mrs. Lambert. I didn't want to buy her ancestral home out from under her . . . But I still wanted it, you understand.

By the end of the afternoon, we were friends. I learned the house had been in her family since the 1880s. Her only son had died young, but she had a grandson named William who was single "just like you, dear. He's very handsome."

I forced a smile. With a gift like mine, dating creates some unusual problems. Once I've met a guy and shaken his hand, how can I ever know if his interest in me is genuine? If I'm attracted to him and I shake his hand, he'll automatically be attracted to me too. That snotty little leprechaun didn't warn me about that! By the time I was halfway through college I had decided to be single for the rest of my life. Useful as my gift is, I'm not interested in a fake relationship.

As I said goodbye to Mrs. Lambert, I shook her hand and said, "You know, I'm a real estate agent. Let me know if you ever decide to sell this place. I might even be interested in it myself."

She shrugged and laughed. "Oh, who'd be interested in a moldering old place like this? It belongs to another century. And it would cost a fortune to fix it up to where I could even sell it."

"I'm in no hurry," I assured her. "But I do think a beautiful old home like this should be preserved."

You see? I didn't press her at all. But two weeks later she made the choice to move into a luxury assisted-living facility. She gladly sold me her home and the surrounding 300 acres for less than a quarter of its market value. I did feel a little guilty about that, but she's the one who suggested the price. I promise.

I continued to visit her for coffee at least once a week, even as I worked on renovating and restoring the house. I truly loved Mrs. Lambert, who now insisted I call her Alice. Just three months after she moved into assisted living, I showed up for our weekly coffee date to be told that she had died of a stroke at dawn that morning. I couldn't believe it. I had been looking forward to showing her over the restored mansion in a few more weeks— maybe even having her come to spend the weekend sometimes.

I made a point of attending the small funeral. I finally saw William, the grandson, in person, though of course I'd seen any number of photos of him. He was indeed handsome—and tall. I wanted nothing from him, so I didn't shake his hand after the graveside service—but it turns out he wanted something from me.

"Is it true you're the lady who bought Granny's house?" he asked.

I nodded.

"I'm going to fight you in court unless you sell that property back to me for exactly what you paid Granny for it," he said pleasantly. "I've been waiting for years to inherit that sublime house and I'm not letting a complete stranger take it away from me. It's our family's home place."

"Your Granny sold it to me legally, and she named the

price. And I assume you inherited all her other assets, including the proceeds of the estate sale."

"I don't know how you did it, but you somehow took advantage of her. You're not getting away with it. She promised me I'd get that house."

"Are you threatening me?" I asked. Now I wished I *had* shaken his hand.

He shrugged. "Call it what you will. I have some persuasive friends. Wherever you are, they'll find you. They won't let you out of their sight until you sell me that house. That was my retirement nest egg."

Mine too, I thought.

As I drove home from the funeral, I couldn't help noticing a nondescript white car that stayed behind me all the way. Seriously? Thank goodness I'd had those fancy iron gates fitted with an electronic lock and opener. I rolled through and watched in the mirror as the gates closed behind me—and the white car inched past my driveway. Through the tinted windows, I could see at least two men inside. Large men.

As soon as I parked the car, I sought out Etienne, the gardener and all-around handyman that had worked for Alice and now worked for me. "Etienne, I have reason to believe someone may be following me and may wish to do me harm. Please do NOT let anyone onto the property and if you see anyone I haven't specifically told you about, call the police."

Etienne gaped at me. "Why would someone want to harm you, Miss Quinn? I don't know what this world is coming to. Would you like me to sleep in the carriage house for a few nights?"

I sighed with relief. That's exactly what I wanted. Etienne was a widower with grown children, so I wouldn't be taking him away from his family, and I knew I'd feel safer with him sleeping in the apartment in the carriage house.

I struggled to fall asleep that night, imagining I heard all kinds of worrisome noises. My uneasy slumber was broken by a noise that wasn't imaginary at all: the sound of breaking glass.

I ran downstairs in my pajamas in time to see a dark figure running down my driveway and away from the house. It appeared to be carrying a baseball bat. Moments later Etienne pounded on my kitchen door. "Miss Quinn! Miss Quinn! Are you all right in there?"

I unlocked the door and let him in. "I'm fine, Etienne. What happened? What broke?"

"All the windows in the carriage house, for one. And when I walked through the garage to get out, I saw that all the windows on your Mustang are broken too. And the hood is bashed in."

I had to sit down. How could sweet little old Alice Lambert's grandson be so menacing? Broken windows could be replaced, but now I felt personally threatened.

I considered my options. Remember that hunky football player I dated in high school? He's a sheriff these days, running the law enforcement in a small community not far from my new house. Maybe I could enlist his help. He's married now, and he's gained quite a bit of weight, but I bet he'd still do anything for me if I shook his hand and asked nicely.

After some strong coffee and scrambled eggs the next morning, I had a mechanic come pick up my car and leave me a loaner to drive while he replaced windows and worked on the hood. Not long afterward I sashayed into Beauregard LeBlanc's office. His face lit up when he saw me. "Riley! How delightful to see you! It's been years, hasn't it?"

I shook his hand and agreed it had been far too long. After a few minutes of chitchat and looking at photos of his two young sons, I came to the point. "Beau, I have a problem and I wonder if you could help me."

"You name it, Riley. You know I'd do almost anything for you."

"A few months ago I bought a house from an old lady who has since died. Now her grandson wants the house and he's hired some Neanderthal muscle to make sure I sell. They sneaked onto my property last night and broke a lot of windows and did some expensive damage to my car. I'm worried for my personal safety."

His face fell. "I'm not sure what I could do without proof, Riley. Do you have security cameras?"

I shook my head, and made a mental note to install cameras as soon as possible.

"I'm sure if we hauled that rat in for questioning he'd claim no knowledge of the vandalism and probably blame it on high-spirited teens. We actually get quite a lot of that, you know—kids who get drunk and roam around bashing mailboxes and cars."

I had an inspiration. "What if you kept me here? You could throw me in jail on a technicality until you've caught those thugs."

Beau's jaw dropped. "You *want* to be in jail? What on earth would I charge you with?"

I slapped him gently on the cheek. "Assaulting a police officer."

He grinned. "I can always withdraw the charges later, I guess. You're under arrest, Riley Quinn."

The jail had only three cells, two of which were empty. The cell farthest away from the door held a drunk, peacefully sleeping it off.

"I won't put you next to that guy," Beau assured me. The cells were separated by metal bars rather than walls. He led me into the nearest cell and rubbed his chin. "I have a feeling you'll be here at least overnight, and I'm sorry. I'll have one of my men stake out your place and watch to see if anyone shows up to do more damage. If someone tries any funny business, I promise you we'll catch them, and once you press charges they'll be properly dealt with."

I hadn't left the house planning to spend the night in jail—that had been a spur-of-the-moment inspiration. Now I wished I'd brought a book to read. "Hey, Beau!" I called. "Got anything to read?"

He brought me a hunting magazine and I had to be content with that. I couldn't complain because being in jail was my idea. The day dragged on and I spent much of it staring at the sky through the tiny window. When night came, I tried to fall asleep despite the bright lighting in my cell.

I had just started to drift off when a commotion arose in the outer office. Sitting up, I waited to see what was going on. I heard muffled voices, doors opening and closing, but nothing that would give me a clue—until the door opened and an officer walked in with a handcuffed William Lambert.

"Look who we found climbing the fence onto your property," said the officer. "He claims he's innocent, but at the very least he was trespassing."

Instead of the death stare I expected, William gave me an agonized look I found hard to interpret.

"Where's Beau?" I asked, thinking he'd come to rescue me now that William was in custody.

"He went home," the officer explained. "He'll be back to deal with this situation in the morning."

Great. William was shoved into the middle cell, and once the door was locked and the officer had left, he walked to the bars between our cells and stared at me.

"It's not what you think," he said. "And what the heck did *you* do to get in here?"

"I had to ask to be put here so I'd be safe from *you*," I huffed. "After your goons broke all those windows and bashed in my Mustang, I figured you were going to send them in to bash *me* next. I don't know how on earth you could be related to sweet Alice Lambert."

"It's true I screwed up big time," he admitted. "But not in the way you think. I was furious when I heard Granny had sold her place to a stranger. I might have gone to a bar and I might have drunk too much and I might have loudly complained about the unfairness of it all. Just blowing off steam, you know?"

I shrugged. I might have blown off steam a time or two myself.

"There were these two guys in the bar who heard me talking and they introduced themselves as Alf and Herb. They said they understood my situation and wanted to help. Both of them are huge and intimidating. I thought if they paid you a visit and encouraged you to sell the house to me, you'd be scared enough to do it. Heck—they scared *me*! I swear that's all I wanted. But they just said, 'Leave her to us. She'll sell, all right.' And I had the distinct impression they expected some sort of payment from me for their trouble."

"So you didn't tell them to vandalize my property?"

"No! In fact I specifically told them *not* to go onto the land and not to touch anything of yours. They were supposed to confront you when you were in town and just use their size and presence to intimidate you. And maybe spray some threatening graffiti on your driveway."

"I'd believe you if it weren't for the fact that you just got caught trespassing on my property."

"I was worried sick about you," he said. "I met up with Alf and Herb for supper and they bragged about what they'd done last night. I realized I was in way over my head and that you might actually get hurt. So yeah, I climbed the fence and was trying to get to the house to make sure you were all right and warn you about Alf and Herb. I wanted to tell you to stay in a hotel until I figured out how to get them to back off. Sure, I want my granny's house—but I don't want to commit a crime to get it and I certainly don't want anyone getting hurt."

I mulled over his words. If he was telling the truth, he was just kind of lame and cowardly—not an actual criminal. In a way, he was a victim himself, of two thugs who took matters into their own hands.

William sat on his cot. "Tell me what you've done to the house."

What else did I have to do? I told him how I'd modernized the bathrooms without losing the historical look; how I'd put in central air conditioning so cleverly that it wasn't obvious at all; how I'd refurbished but kept the old gas lights instead of replacing them with electric fixtures. He listened eagerly and asked intelligent questions. The longer we talked, the more I realized that in a lot of ways, we were on the same wavelength. We both had a passion for historical buildings and wanted to preserve them.

Against my own wishes, I found myself liking him. Not enough to sell him the house, obviously—but I invited him to take a tour when I had finished all my renovations.

He cleared his throat. "That might be difficult to schedule if I am rotting in jail."

I shrugged.

"Can I ask you a personal question?" he said.

I said nothing. I hate personal questions.

"Granny always told me that the only way she'd ever leave that house was feet first. I'm trying to imagine how on earth you or anyone could have changed her mind."

I breathed a sigh of relief and told the truth. "We struck up a friendship and she invited me for coffee. When I saw that house I couldn't believe it. I'm in the real estate business and I let her know I was interested. I didn't press her in any way. But maybe just mentioning it got her thinking that she might be more comfortable in a smaller place. It was all her idea."

He rubbed his chin thoughtfully. "That's the truth? You were her friend and she offered you the house of her own accord?"

I nodded.

His next words surprised me. "Thank you."

"For what?" How had we gone from threats to thankfulness?

"For being Granny's friend. For being a sympathetic listener. For caring about her house. I hated thinking of her moldering away by herself in that fabulous house. I'm glad you brightened the last few months of her life. I should have come to visit more often."

I struggled with my feelings. I was becoming very fond of this man. In many ways he seemed like a kindred spirit. But could I trust him?

"Are you still going to fight me for the house?" I asked.

He shook his head. "No. What a stupid idea that was. And I realize now that it's in good hands. You're very skilled at what you do, Riley Quinn. You have something—I don't know what it is—something very persuasive about you. If you don't press charges and we both get out of here, I could see us working together. Finding old historic houses and giving them a new life—for a profit, of course."

"Of course!" I agreed. I hadn't been this attracted to a man in ten years. I wouldn't mind at all working with such a like-minded partner.

"You know," he said, "Granny has a sister, and she's rich too. My great-aunt Helena. She married money and she has a classy mansion that would make a great investment property."

I grinned at him. "What are you suggesting?"

"I think you know what I'm suggesting. Withdraw the charges against me. We'll make a great team. Here, shake my hand and we'll call it a deal." He thrust his right hand through the bars.

I had to think fast. What if this was my one and only genuine chance at future happiness? I made my choice.

"I have a weird custom," I said. "When I'm really serious about something, I always shake with my left hand."

The End

The Book on the Road

W ind rustled through the treetops as a solitary man walked along the dirt road in the glimmering light before dawn. His clothes were well worn and he carried a leather knapsack on his back. As the light around him grew, he reached a crossroads. A smaller, narrower road branched off from the one he had been following. A signpost pointing toward the new road read "Paradise," bringing a smile to his thin face.

He sat down, leaned against the signpost, and enjoyed some bread and cheese from his knapsack. When he finished his meal, he drew something else from his bag—a largish book. Bound in leather, it had an intricate knot design on its green cover. He flipped through it, his eyes lingering on the exquisite illustrations and old-fashioned typeface. With a sigh, he sought a specific page.

"I think this will do nicely," he murmured. He laid the open book down on the very edge of the road he'd been walking on. Then he stood up, gathered his things, and set off along the smaller road. "I've always wanted to see Paradise," he said.

Much later that same day, Jinnia Thakkery rode her horse Blackjack along the same road. After Jinnia had begged them for days, her parents gave permission for her to ride the ten miles to visit her cousin Aivlynn. She had promised to return the following day, but for now she urged Blackjack to trot faster and faster. The sooner she reached her uncle's house, the longer she and Aivlynn would have together.

She saw the crossroads up ahead and spied something lying near the signpost: a book. Curious, she reined in her horse and stopped to look. The book looked old, and lay open right beside the road. After dismounting, she picked it up, and as she did so a strange sensation spread from her hands to her whole body. The page had a title: Chapter XX.

The first sentence of the first paragraph read, "Jinnia paused to pick up the book and started reading, little knowing how her life would change."

Jinnia's eyes widened in shock. At first she thought the book happened to be about a girl named Jinnia who also happened to find a book beside the road—then she read the next sentence. "Blackjack stamped his hooves impatiently." She stared at Blackjack, who stamped his hooves. "This is unreal," Jinnia told him. Then she noticed the illustration on the facing page—a girl on a black horse by a crossroads. It was a very good likeness of her and Blackjack. After slamming the book shut, she stuck it into one of her saddlebags and sprang back into the saddle. Blackjack continued on down the road, but Jinnia had lost her sense of urgency to reach her cousin. She pulled the book out and it popped open at the same page.

"Jinnia had no way of knowing," she read, "that a young boy in the forest was in desperate need of her help." Ridiculous though it might be, Jinnia scanned the forest on either side of the road. No young boy appeared, in need of help or otherwise. She tried to turn the page of the book, but it would not open to any other.

"The boy had hidden in a hollow tree," she read.

She slid the book back into her saddlebag. "Blackjack, I guess we're going to go looking for a hollow tree." She hadn't exactly forgotten about her cousin, but this mystery intrigued her. She inspected the trees on each side of the road. She needed to find a tree large enough for someone to hide in. Blackjack advanced uncertainly, lacking guidance from her.

She had gone perhaps half a mile when something bright caught her attention. It seemed to be hanging from the low branch of a large shrub some twenty feet or so to the left of the road. She had to dismount to walk through the heavy undergrowth and look at it. A bulging red leather sack swung from a sturdy leather drawstring. When she grabbed it, the weight surprised her. Could it be gold?

No, when she opened the bag she found only a set of marbles, a child's plaything—but these marbles were like none she'd ever seen. They were quite a bit larger than normal and made of stone rather than glass—black stone with shining golden flecks, polished to a mirror-like shine and perfectly spherical. "These are some pretty fancy marbles," she told Blackjack. "I bet they belong to some rich kid who won't even miss them."

She tucked them into her saddlebag and resumed her search for large trees. She didn't bother looking at the book because she hadn't even found the boy who needed her help yet, and she had a feeling the page wouldn't turn until she found the boy. Some ten minutes later she looked up on her right toward a low green mound crowned with huge old oak trees. That looked promising. No path appeared through the undergrowth, so she dismounted yet again and led Blackjack toward the trees, bending plants and shrubs to the side to make room.

When they reached the nearest tree, she tied Blackjack to one of its protruding branches and proceeded cautiously on foot. She circled the first tree and found it solid. Moving toward the next tree, she stopped every few steps to listen. As she approached the fourth tree, she heard it. Whimpering. Heavy breathing.

Making as little noise as possible, she inched her way around the tree. There. The tree was hollow, and jammed into the hollow space crouched a young boy of perhaps eight or nine, with tears streaming from his startling blue eyes and making tracks on his dirty cheeks.

"Are you going to kill me?" he asked. His voice quavered.

She knelt down beside him, wanting nothing more than to give him a big hug. "Why on earth would I want to hurt you at all?"

"Everybody else wants to kill me," he whispered.

She smiled. "I'm somebody, and I just want to be your friend," she said. "My name is Jinnia. What's yours?"

He blinked tears from his eyes with long dark eyelashes and peered up at her. "Gil."

Poor child. She couldn't imagine why anyone would want to kill him, but he clearly believed it. "Are you lost, Gil?"

He nodded. "And I don't know where to go and I'm in big trouble because I lost Grandfather's marbles."

She heaved a sigh of relief. "I think I can help you, Gil. I'll take you on my big black horse and we'll go to my uncle's house. I'm sure we'll be able to get you back with your family. And guess what? I just found some marbles. I bet they're yours."

His face brightened and he followed her without complaint back to where Blackjack waited. "Were they in a red bag?" he asked.

"Yes, and I promise you shall have them as soon as we

get you to my uncle's house." She felt she had to have some kind of leverage to ensure his cooperation.

"It's a good thing Blackjack is so strong," she said as she settled young Gil in front of her on the saddle. They struggled to get through the undergrowth and back to the road, but once they did, Jinnia pushed Blackjack to a canter.

"I still don't understand why you think someone wants to kill you," she said. "Kids lose things all the time and no one wants to kill them over it."

"I was visiting Grandfather," Gil said. His voice sounded a little breathless due to the motion of the horse. "Some bad men rode up on horses, then they came and banged on the door. Grandfather gave me his marbles and lifted me out the back window. He told me to run and not look back and to keep the marbles safe. And he told me if any of those men found me they would kill me!"

This story seemed a little far-fetched to Jinnia, unless . . . "What is your Grandfather's name?" she asked.

Gil giggled. "Grandfather!"

Jinnia rolled her eyes, glad that Gil couldn't see her. "Okay, smarty-pants. What do Grandfather's friends call him?"

"Most people call him Sir, but his best friends call him Majesterion."   .

A visceral shudder wracked Jinnia's body and for the first time since finding the book fear threatened to undo her. Majesterion was the most powerful sorcerer in the entire country—and now she had no doubt that the "marbles" were in fact the Orbs of Oraculon, which many people would indeed kill for. What kind of adventure had that book got her into?

She reigned Blackjack in and pulled out the book again. This time the page turned easily and revealed another picture of her on Blackjack with Gil in front of her. The paragraph below began, "As Jinnia and young Gil raced toward her cousin's house, their five pursuers began closing in on them. Jinnia knew her only hope of surviving was to surrender and give up the Orbs."

She slammed the book shut. Even she knew it could be disastrous if the Orbs fell into the wrong hands. Stupid book. "We're going to gallop now," she told Gil. "Hang on tight!"

Blackjack was far from fresh but he broke into a gallop just as she heard hoof-beats on the road behind her. She looked back and saw three men on horseback gaining on her. *Ha!* She thought. *The book said there would be five!* Then she rounded a curve in the road and saw two more mounted men waiting and blocking the road far ahead.

Desperately, she looked to both sides and realized the thick undergrowth made it impossible to turn aside in either direction.

"Those are the bad men!" Gil yelled, looking ahead.

Jinnia reached into her saddlebag, groping for the bag of marbles. She had no time to consult the book and her only hope was to use the Orbs. She had no idea how they worked but she had to try. She had never been out of the Forest in her life, but she'd heard of a place called Cobalt Bay, which bordered a large body of water. In the split second she had to decide, that exotic place sprang to mind. She had already loosed the drawstring of the bag and slowed Blackjack to a trot. Now, using every ounce of strength she had, she threw the heavy marbles ahead of Blackjack, whispering "Cobalt Bay" as she did so.

The sixteen Orbs did not fall to the ground as anyone would expect such heavy missiles to do. Instead, they scattered in the air until they formed a perfect vertical circle on the road a few feet ahead, like a round door. The circle was large enough for a horse to go through. "Come on," she told Gil. "Bend down over the horse's neck." The men in front were less than a stone's throw away and the men behind sounded very close.

As Gil obeyed her instruction, she bent forward over him and Blackjack trotted right through the circle of orbs.

Her eyes slammed shut in response to the bright light that hit her like a blow. Blackjack stopped moving. Gil breathed heavily but didn't say anything. Jinnia opened her eyes, squinting against the light.

Having only known the filtered light in the Forest all her life, Jinnia had no idea that sunlight could be so strong and bright. The three of them now stood on a wide beach of pale blue sand, which curved around in a huge half circle, bordering a massive deep blue body of water. She had heard of the ocean but never imagined she'd ever see it.

The Orbs! Where were they? She turned Blackjack around and saw the orbs had dropped to the sand in a disorganized pile. Breathing a sigh of relief, she dismounted and helped Gil down. "See?" she said. "We've still got your grandfather's marbles. Let's put them back in the bag for now."

How had she known what to do? Had the Orbs somehow told her?

"Where are we?" Gil asked. "Is that the sea?"

Jinnia nodded. "I think so. I've never been here myself, but I think we're in a place called Cobalt Bay. If you look on the other side of the water maybe you can see some buildings. That must be the town of Cobalt."

"How did we get here?"

She put the bag of marbles back into her saddlebag. "Did you not know your grandfather's marbles are magic? That's why those bad men wanted them. They can form a kind of door to take you anywhere you want to go in our whole country—maybe the whole world. Your grandfather and his marbles are very famous. There's a reason so many people just call him 'Sir.'"

"That must be why Phinn is so respectful and obedient around Grandfather," Gil said. "He's not like that with anyone else. And he has to be respectful anyway because he's Grandfather's apprentice too."

Jinnia laughed. "And who is Phinn?"

"My big brother. He and my sister Beryl take care of me since our parents died. We live a couple of miles from Grandfather's house."

"I am so sorry about your parents," she said. "How about if we walk toward the town? We can even wade in the water if you want. It's so hot here."

Grinning at each other, they sat down to remove their boots and socks. Once everything had been stowed, Jinnia took Blackjack's reins and led him to the water. He sniffed it hopefully, took an experimental swallow, and spit it out.

"I don't think that water is good for horses," Gil said. "It's good for boys' feet though!"

The three of them splashed through the shallows as they walked around the rim of the bay toward the town. Even Blackjack seemed to enjoy the cool water on his legs. As they walked, Jinnia thought hard about their situation. Now she knew how to use the Orbs, she could get back to the Forest at any time—but what would be the point? Those men would be waiting. She certainly didn't want to lead them to her uncle's house or her own home. Then she remembered the book. They were about halfway to the town of Cobalt.

"Let's stop for a minute and have a snack," she said. "I need to look at my book again."

She pulled out a nosebag for Blackjack and some bread for Gil. Then she lifted the book out of the saddlebag and leaned against Blackjack's warm flank as she opened it. The picture on this page showed the three of them standing in the blue water with the pale blue sand of the beach curving before and behind them.

"Jinnia's rash use of the Orbs saved her life," she read, "but at what cost? Now she found herself stranded in a seaside community where she didn't know anyone. Her chances of retaining the Orbs and protecting herself and the boy were not very good unless she could find someone trustworthy who might help her. It would be wiser for her to return to the forest and get help from her family."

Jinnia slammed the book shut again and returned it to her saddlebag. She was starting to hate that book. Nothing could make her go back and endanger her family. She smiled at Gil. "I don't suppose you know anyone who lives on the coast, do you?"

"Only my other grandparents," he said. "My grandfather is a fisherman somewhere, so he must live near the sea."

"Do you know what town?"

He shook his head. An idea began to form in Jinnia's mind.

"Do you know your grandparents' names?" she asked. "Their real names?"

"I don't know my grandfather's name because Grandmother always just calls him 'Dear." But he calls her Trilla sometimes. And there's a sign on my grandfather's trunk that says 'Bakersmith.'"

"How would you feel about trying to use the marbles to visit your grandparents?"

"I've never been to their house. They always come visit us. Can we go there please?"

"We can give it a try."

Jinnia took the Orbs out again and led Blackjack out onto the hot dry sand, with Gil trailing close behind. She threw the Orbs into the air, saying "Trilla Bakersmith." Again they formed a large circle in the air, and Jinnia led the three of them through it.

She stumbled for a moment after passing through the Orbs. The sand had disappeared and now they stood on a rocky path. When she turned around to gather up the Orbs, she saw Cobalt Bay behind her now. They stood on a steep hill marking the mouth of the bay and looking down on the town from the north side. A cozy blue and white cottage sat a few yards from them at the end of a crushed seashell-lined path.

"Looks like we might want to put our boots back on," she said. Soon they were walking on the path to the house. Jinnia tied Blackjack to a tree that leaned over a quiet little pond where he could get a drink. She realized she felt very thirsty herself and wondered if she had any water left in her water skin.

The two of them walked up the stairs to the blue porch and Jinnia rang the large brass bell hanging next to the bright blue door. A dog barked and kept on barking until someone said, "My goodness, Fletch, stop that nonsense!"

The door opened and a middle-aged lady found herself under attack by an ecstatic Gil, who hugged her ferociously. She laughed and hugged him back, and Jinnia found herself liking Trilla Bakersmith before she even opened her mouth.

"Come inside, you two!" she said, then, "I don't know who you are, but thank you for bringing my grandson to me. I had no notice that he was coming for a visit."

Gil jumped up and down as they followed her into the house. "I almost got killed, Grandmother! Some bad men came to my other grandfather's house and he helped me escape! Then Jinnia found me and saved me from those bad men using nothing but Grandfather's marbles!"

The grandmother looked sharply up at Jinnia, who acknowledged the look with a nod. "Are the marbles safe?" she asked.

Again, Jinnia nodded. A large parchment map tacked up on the dining room wall caught her attention then, and she stepped forward to examine it. She had never seen such a large and detailed map of Ormagon and the waters and islands to the west of it. The only maps she'd seen in the Forest were maps of the Forest itself. On this map, the Forest covered a large section of the northeast of the country, but still less than a third of the total land area. Cobalt Bay lay much farther south and on the coast of the Sunset Ocean. It would be a long journey home if she had to make it without the help of the Orbs. But she noticed that the location of the fabled sorcerers' stronghold of Hightower was marked, located not too far east of the town of Cobalt. Perhaps Hightower could offer safety for the Orbs and for her and Gil.

Minutes later, the three of them sat around a charming table on the porch, with fresh cold water to drink and a tray piled high with snacks to choose from. The blue sea sparkled down below them, beyond the deep blue tile roofs of the town.

"Your grandfather will be so sorry to have missed you," Trilla said to Gil. "He's out fishing with his crew and I don't expect him back for at least a couple of weeks."

Jinnia heaved a quiet sigh of relief. If Gil had known his grandfather's first name, she would have said that first and the Orbs would have deposited them in the sea somewhere. This peaceful cottage was a much better option. When they had eaten and drunk their fill, Trilla said, "Gil, if you go down the path on the other side of the house, you'll reach a tiny beach that often has some lovely seashells. Could you go look for me? I love to use them as decorations."

Gil's eyes lit up and he went in search of the path at once, with the dog Fletch as company. As soon as they were out of earshot, Trilla turned to Jinnia with a serious expression on her face.

"What can you tell me? Is Majesterion still alive? Who are these men who attacked? How do you know my grandson? How did you know how to use the Orbs? Why did you come here?"

Jinnia took a deep breath. "I don't know the fate of Majesterion, I don't know who the bad men are, I found Gil in a hollow tree after reading about him in a book, the Orbs showed me how to use them, and I came here because I don't know anyone in Cobalt and Gil and I need help."

"Sensible girl," Trilla answered. "What's all this about a book?"

"I found it in the road," Jinnia explained, "and I've decided it's a stupid book. It wanted me to give the Orbs to those awful men!"

"What are the odds," Trilla mused, "that a teenage girl would find the Tome of Destiny and the Orbs of Oraculon in the same day?"

"The Tome of Destiny?"

"Yes, that book has been around for decades, maybe longer. The Keeper of the book leaves it lying open someplace where it will be found, and opens it to a chapter that will be about the finder's life. Some of the stories are sad and some have happy endings, I've heard—but the book never lets you read ahead to the end of the story."

Jinnia snorted. "I've noticed."

Trilla gave her a questioning look and Jinnia walked back to Blackjack to retrieve the book. She wasn't sure she wanted Trilla to see the page unless she got a look at it first, so she stood beside her horse and opened it.

It opened to a page with a picture of Trilla's quaint little cottage, with her and Jinnia sitting at the table on the porch. "Trilla truly loved her grandson," Jinnia read, "but she also desired to have the Orbs for herself, so that her husband could use them to escape possible shipwreck or a pirate attack. Even as she offered hospitality to Jinnia, she plotted to get the Orbs from her."

Jinnia closed the book slowly, returned it to the

saddlebag, and plodded back to the cottage, her mind racing. She couldn't let Trilla know she suspected her, but at the same time she had to figure out a way to leave while she still had the Orbs.

"I thought you were going to bring the book to show me," Trilla said as she approached.

"There's nothing about what happens next," Jinnia said. "It just shows that we made it safely to your house— but it hinted we wouldn't be here for long."

"Oh?" Trilla's eyebrows rose. "Why shouldn't you stay as long as you want? I'm sure Gil would love to see his grandfather when he returns from his fishing trip."

"I'm sure he would too. But he made a promise to his other grandfather and I want to help him keep it."

A look of intense annoyance flitted across the older woman's face, but she managed to suppress it as Gil came bounding around the corner of the house with hands full of seashells. "Do you like them?" he asked as he laid them out along the railing of the porch.

She smiled warmly at him. "I love them. I knew you'd find some beautiful shells. Your eyes are so much better at finding things than mine are."

Jinnia looked at Gil. "Gil, those men who were after you—do you think they knew who you were? Did they know you are Majesterion's grandson?"

He nodded. "When they banged on the door, they said, 'We know you're in there and we know you've got no one to protect you except your grandson--who is only a child.'"

Inwardly Jinnia relaxed a little. Now she had a convincing reason to leave and take Gil with her. "I'm afraid we can't stay here then," she said, looking from Gil to Trilla.

"What do you mean?" Trilla demanded.

"If those men, whoever they are, know that Gil is Majesterion's grandson, how long do you think it will be before they find out who his other relatives are? It won't take them long to zero in on this house."

Trilla's face paled. "Do you think I'm in danger?"

Jinnia stood up. "Not if Gil and I aren't here. I'm afraid we need to leave at once."

She watched the conflicting emotions come and go on Trilla's face. In the end, her love for her grandson won out over her greed. "Let me load you up with as much food and water as you can carry," she said. "Do you have any idea where you'll go next?"

"I have an idea," Jinnia said, "but you realize it would be dangerous for me to tell you."

Trilla's face fell. "You're right. I should have realized that."

Minutes later, Jinnia and a rather sulky Gil were back in the saddle. "We could have at least stayed for supper," he said.

Jinnia could hardly tell him she was trying to protect the Orbs from his own grandmother. "Well, at least she sent a tasty supper for us to eat on the road," she replied.

"Where are we going, anyway? We can't go back to the Forest and we can't go to Cobalt town if the bad men find out that my grandmother lives here."

"You're absolutely right," Jinnia agreed. "I got a look at the map in the cottage and the only thing that makes sense is for us to go straight to Hightower. Your grandfather's fellow sorcerers have the means to protect us and the marbles."

"Can't we use the marbles to get there?" Gil asked.

Jinnia thought about it. Now that she'd had time to consider the matter, she had some reservations about using the Orbs. "Sure, we could. But I wonder if using them might somehow alert someone to what we are doing and where we are going. There are bad sorcerers as well as good ones, you know. What if they have a way of tracking the Orbs when someone uses them?"

"I wish there weren't so many bad people in the world," Gil huffed. "I'm so tired of riding."

Jinnia hoped her concerns could be chalked up to excess paranoia, but she kept Blackjack to a slow trot as they traveled through the lush fields and pastures of Ormagon, going always eastward.

Over the next three days, Jinnia tried to make riding and camping fun for Gil. She missed her own family and wondered what they thought had happened to her. Would she ever see them again?

On the morning of the fourth day, as the Central Mountains loomed up before them, they saw another horse headed toward them from the north. It was too late to hide, and they were in open country anyway. Gil leaned back against Jinnia. "If it's one of those bad men, we're going to have to use the marbles," he said.

Jinnia kept Blackjack walking toward the mountains as if she had nothing to fear. No point in galloping unless it became necessary. At the same time, though, she reached into her saddlebag and closed her hand on the leather bag containing the Orbs.

"Look at the rider," she said to Gil. "Let me know if it looks like any of the men who were after you."

A moment later, Gil startled her by shrieking with delight. "It's not a bad man! It's my brother Phinn!"

The rider soon caught up with them and Jinnia found herself being introduced to Phinn, a tall young man who looked like an older and more handsome version of Gil.

"Thank heaven you're safe," he said to Gil. "I should never have left Grandfather undefended, even though it was he who sent me on my errand."

"Is Grandfather all right?"

Phinn nodded. "He's fine. He knew an enchantment that enabled him to escape and go to Hightower, but he came close to failing."

Jinnia was puzzled. "Why didn't he just use the Orbs? He could have taken Gil with him and we could have been spared all the trouble of the last few days."

Phinn stayed silent for a moment before answering. "You've taken good care of my brother, and you've protected the Orbs, so I will have to trust you to keep this secret. The Orbs are limited. Each person who uses them, whether for good or ill, can only use them thirteen times. Grandfather reached the limit some years ago, but maybe you can see why he would not want this information to be widely known."

"How many times have you used them?" Gil asked.

"None. They are only to be used in moments of extremity," Phinn replied.

"Ha!" Gil said. "We've used them twice!"

Phinn looked at Jinnia, and she nodded. "I would consider both times to be moments of extremity," she said, and then told him the story of their escape.

Phinn nodded thoughtfully. "What does the Tome say will happen next?" he asked.

Jinnia hadn't looked at the book since they'd left the cottage. She trusted it less and less. Did she even know if Gil's grandmother had wanted the Orbs? No. What if the book lied?"

She pulled the book out of the saddlebag and opened it with a sigh. "Jinnia unwisely trusted Phinn, knowing nothing about him," she read silently, "and not knowing that someday she would make the bigger mistake of marrying him. Her mission was in danger and her best hope lay in using the Orbs to escape from Phinn and get to Hightower."

She slammed the book shut. "Stupid book," she said.

Sooner or later, she *had* to trust someone. And over the last few days, Gil had told her enough about his big brother to convince her that he could be trusted. She had no intention of marrying him, of course, but that didn't mean she couldn't trust him to help protect her and Gil and the orbs.

Phinn's eyebrows rose. "You don't like what it said?"

"Well, no. But I think it is right in saying we need to get to Hightower as soon as possible."

"Agreed. We're about twenty miles away now. Is your horse up to cantering?"

For answer, she dug her heels into Blackjack's flanks and took off at a canter. Phinn easily caught up with her. "Hey," he said, "we're working together now, remember? We're much safer if we stay together."

She nodded, still angry at the book. She knew it wasn't as infallible as some might think. She had defied it twice already.

An hour later, they had reached the mountains and could see the golden spires of Hightower in the distance, perched on a tall green hill. Jinnia couldn't quite explain why, but she found it impossible to resist glancing over at Phinn every few minutes. And every time she did, he was already looking at her. It made her uncomfortable.

Distracted as she was, Gil startled her when he yelled, "The bad men found us!"

Phinn glanced northward, and Jinnia followed his gaze to see eleven men on horseback galloping in their direction through a flat-bottomed ravine.

"I am so sorry," Phinn said. "They must have had someone watching me, and now they've followed me to you and Gil. If their horses are fresh, we don't have any chance of getting away from them."

They both urged their tired horses to a gallop, but Jinnia knew they wouldn't be able to keep it up all the way to Hightower. Soon she heard the hoof beats of the pursuing horses.

"Should I use the Orbs?" she yelled across to Phinn.

He glanced behind at their pursuers, then ahead, as if judging how far they could get toward Hightower before being overtaken.

The high thin sound of a ram's horn drifted toward them and superseded the sound of galloping horses. Puzzled, Jinnia looked ahead and saw the last thing she would have expected—an army of knights on horseback with shiny gold helmets and long lances. There were at least a hundred of them, and they were on a collision course toward Jinnia, Gil, and Phinn. They divided, thundered past on either side, and continued on to engage the pursuing men.

Jinnia and Phinn slowed their horses to a walk, and both craned their necks around to see the knights make short work of the enemy. "Who are those knights?" Jinnia asked. "Where did they come from?"

Phinn grinned at her. "That's the Hightower Guard. Grandfather must have foreseen our arrival—and the fact that we'd be in danger. He and the other sorcerers sent the guard to ensure our safety."

Minutes later, the guard surrounded them and escorted them the remaining couple of miles to Hightower. As they rode in through the gates, a tall man with grey hair greeted them. Gil jumped from the saddle and into the old man's arms. Majesterion held him tight and looked up at Jinnia, his eyes bright with tears.

"Thank you for keeping my grandson safe," he said. "I don't understand how you got involved, but I am so grateful."

"She's got the Tome of Destiny and the Orbs," Phinn said. "I'm sure you'll want to hear all about it."

"Indeed I do."

Jinnia became increasingly impatient over the next three days, although she enjoyed touring Hightower and meeting so many powerful enchanters. All of them thanked her for keeping the Orbs safe. Ramillia, one of the few woman sorcerers, called her aside for a private meeting. "I would like to offer you a place as my apprentice," she said. "You have shown courage and loyalty and common sense. Everything else you need can be learned. There are so few of us women—I'd love to have you join us."

Jinnia couldn't help being tempted. Her experience using the Orbs had piqued her interest in the art of sorcery— as long as it was "white" rather than "black." She liked the idea of using magic to help others, as she had helped Gil.

"I'm only sixteen," she said. "I will have to return home and ask my parents' permission."

Ramillia nodded. "You can return home to the Forest with Majesterion and his family. If you decide to accept my offer, ask Majesterion to contact me and I will send an escort of Guards for you."

During the long ride home to the Forest, Jinnia found herself enjoying Phinn's company more and more. She was already attached to Gil, and Majesterion, the famous and powerful enchanter, seemed more like a kindly grandfather to her. She was glad he lived in the Forest not too far from her family's home. Already, she couldn't help wondering if Phinn might come to visit her sometime.

She realized she hadn't looked at the book for days, and only when Phinn brought it up. "Does your book say we will reach our homes safely?" he asked.

"I don't know and I don't care," she said. "I'd rather just take life as it comes."

"Smart girl," Majesterion said.

Phinn cleared his throat. "I, uh, was hoping that maybe it would tell you we're going to get married someday," he said.

She felt her face heating up from embarrassment. "Why would it tell me that?"

"Because the morning I met you, I tossed my divining dice to see if I would successfully reach Hightower. And what the dice indicated instead was that I would meet my future wife and that she'd be with someone precious to me."

"So that's why you kept staring at me."

Majesterion roared with laughter. "I could have told you that the first time I saw you two together."

"The book is stupid," Jinnia said. "I don't have to marry anyone if I don't want to."

Phinn's face became serious. "No, of course you don't. But over the next few years I'll work hard at making you want to. And if you go to work with Ramillia—just think. We'll be an unbeatable team."

"You already are," Gil said.

The following day they reached the Forest and the day after that, when Jinnia looked ahead, she saw the crossroads where she had found the book a couple of weeks ago—weeks that felt like a lifetime. She pointed it out to Majesterion. "Can I just put it back where I found it?" she asked. "I don't like this book."

"Yes, by all means," he said. "The Keeper is bound to be somewhere nearby. But I suggest you look to see what the book has to say about this adventure you've been on."

Sitting in the saddle, Jinnia opened the book one last time. The picture showed the four of them on horseback next to the signpost. "Jinnia was well on her way to becoming one of the most skilled enchanters in Ormagon," she read, "and above all she learned to trust her own judgment instead of slavishly following the advice of a magic book she happened to find on the road."

She dismounted and laid the book down beside the signpost. As she swung back into the saddle, she grinned at her companions. "I hope I never see that book again," she said. "I prefer to write my own story."

The End

L. M. Burklin

The Girl in the Park

"Is there a smudge on my nose?"

Michael shook his head.

"Why are you staring at me?"

"Because I like your face."

She laughed. He loved her laugh. It was so musical and infectious. He wished his lunch hour would last forever. On this spectacular spring day in Stone Mountain Park, he barely noticed the natural beauty around him because he had eyes only for Kathleen. Her strawberry blonde hair and roguish green eyes charmed him almost as much as the deep dimples in each cheek. He worked at making her smile just so he could see her dimples.

"Have you ever seen the laser show?" she asked.

"Tons of times. Since I work here, I can stay for the show whenever I want."

"Maybe you could stay to see the show sometime this summer," she said, "and I could stay too, and we could watch it together."

"I'd like that," he said. His heart leapt. She wanted to keep seeing him!

Anxiety crept in later while he ate supper with his mother.

"Michael Mahoney," she said, "what on earth are you thinking of? You haven't heard a word I've said for the last five minutes."

"Kathleen wants to watch the laser show with me this summer," he said.

"And you're going to chicken out, aren't you?"

"I know I shouldn't let it bother me, Mother, but I'm about the age now that Dad was when he disappeared."

"So? You're also about the same age as your grandfather was when he disappeared in Ireland. But you can't live your life in fear, or I'll never be a grandmother! Why don't you invite Kathleen home for dinner?"

"A lady who's so eager for grandchildren might scare her off," he said with a smile.

The next day Kathleen was waiting for him when he took his lunch break. She looked so bohemian with her long denim skirt, tie-dyed T-shirt, and a bright green sash setting off her trim waist. They found a shady spot to sit.

"My mother sent an extra meat pie today," he said. He felt himself flushing. "Would you like it? I feel awful eating in front of you."

She smiled as she accepted the pastry. "I love meat pies," she said. "But why do you still live with your mother? I'm younger than you and I live all by myself."

He wrenched his attention away from her very attractive curves. "Well, my father, uh, died when I was six. I did move out after college, but last year when Mother broke her hip, I moved her in with me. She gets around a lot better now, but I enjoy her company."

Kathleen smiled. "Doesn't that put a damper on your relationships?"

He laughed to cover his embarrassment, not knowing what to say. A young woman in a floppy hat and huge sunglasses walked up and stopped in front of them, fiddling with her fancy camera before taking several pictures of the carving on the rock face.

"Sorry if I blocked your view," she said, turning toward them with a smile. "Would you like me to snap your picture? I can put it up on Facebook or email it to you."

Kathleen's reaction startled Michael.

"No!" she said sharply. "I don't like photographs."

The girl shrugged and walked on down the path, snapping photos as she went.

"What was that about?" Michael asked.

"She's creepy, that's all. I don't want her taking my picture. It's an invasion of privacy."

The conversation moved on, but a few minutes later Michael glanced up and saw Sunglass Girl again. She was on the other side of the huge lawn, still taking pictures—but she seemed to be aiming at Kathleen and himself. He didn't say anything, considering how Kathleen felt about photos, but his curiosity went into overdrive.

That evening while he was washing dishes, the doorbell rang and his mother answered it.

"Michael, dear," she called, "you have a visitor."

His heart stopped. Kathleen? How could she know where he lived? Why would she come here?

He dried his hands and walked to the living room on trembling legs. It wasn't Kathleen. This woman was taller, with auburn hair and deep blue eyes. She held out her hand.

"Mr. Mahoney?"

"Yes." She had a firm handshake, and seemed reluctant to let his hand go.

"Agent Molly McBride," she said.

She showed him her I.D. "Federal Bureau of Investigation. SNB division."

"FBI?" he said. "You've got the wrong guy. All I do is work at the museum in Stone Mountain Park and then come home and hang out with my mom."

"Relax," Agent McBride said. "You're not the target of an investigation, though it might have looked that way in the park this afternoon."

"You're Sunglass Girl from the park today?"

She grinned. "Well, I prefer Molly. I believe your picnic companion is an SNB that we've been after for years. SNB stands for 'supernatural being.'"

"Kathleen?"

"So she's calling herself Kathleen now, is she? Surely, Mr. Mahoney, you're Irish enough to know about the Little People. Faeries, some call them. Most are content to live in their underground communities, but some, like your friend Kathleen, are predators."

He couldn't help laughing.

"This is the most ridiculous thing I've ever heard of."

Still, he felt a thrill of danger—and uncertainty.

"Has she ever mentioned her age? Offered you food? Has she ever told you she loves you or invited you to her home? Have you ever seen her outside the park, or known her to wear or touch anything made of iron or steel?"

"We've only been meeting for a couple of weeks!"

"Good! I hope that means you are not emotionally invested in the relationship yet and that you will be willing to work with us. Over the years eleven people have disappeared in Stone Mountain Park, and we think your friend Kathleen is responsible. We can't apprehend her, though, unless we witness her in the act of trying to abduct someone. Obviously none of her victims have been able to tell us what happened to them."

"So, you want to use me as bait to catch Kathleen?"

"Well, I hate to put it that way, but . . . yes."

Michael had a whole weekend to ponder what he had

heard before he saw Kathleen again. He spent hours researching faeries on the Internet. It seemed so silly—so surreal. Faeries? In Stone Mountain Park? He went shopping at a reenactment supply place and purchased a few items that he thought might be useful. Part of him hated it. How could sweet, innocent Kathleen be a vicious killer? Maybe the whole thing was a colossal practical joke.

Molly had said all he had to do was keep meeting up with Kathleen and wait for her to make her move. To make things worse, his mother now began scheming to match him up with Molly. He ate lunch with Kathleen every day, watching for suspicious behavior. She never mentioned having a job, and always changed the subject when he asked about her family. But she was sweet and kind and funny, and he couldn't believe she would harm him.

After work he would go home, to find that Mother had invited Molly for dinner.

"I think Kathleen is a good faery," he told Molly.

"There is no such thing as a good faery," Molly retorted. "Don't you understand? They don't have feelings —not like you do. If Kathleen is being kind to you, it's just because you happen to amuse her for the time being."

He clenched his teeth and said nothing. Molly ruffled his hair.

"I don't want you to get hurt."

He smiled back, touched by Molly's concern.

"She reminds me of someone," he told his mother after Molly left one evening. "I can't figure out who."

"It'll come to you when you least expect it," Mother said. "She's a fine Irish girl—maybe she reminds you of one of your cousins."

Two weeks later when he walked Molly to her car after yet another dinner at his apartment, she surprised him by wrapping her arms around his neck and kissing him on the lips.

"What was that for?" he asked when he had caught his breath. Kathleen was much less demonstrative, though she did let him help her up from the grass when they ate on the lawn.

"That's for being such a good sport," she said. "You've been so cooperative. I know I'm not supposed to get emotionally involved, but I just can't resist you, Michael Mahoney."

He stood in the parking lot trembling from head to foot after she drove off. What was going on? Twenty-seven years of being invisible to women, and now he had two very lovely ladies all but throwing themselves at him. The only problem was that the one he cared most deeply for was a heartless killer, and the one who had just kissed him wanted him to lead the other one into a trap.

By May, though he still met Kathleen for lunch every day, he spent many of his evenings with Molly. There were more kisses, all initiated by her. She was the smart choice, the one his mother liked—and she obviously wanted him. But Kathleen made him feel so safe and happy. She seemed to understand his loneliness in a way that Molly couldn't, and he wanted to protect her, somehow.

"The laser show is starting again this weekend," Kathleen said one day. "Are you going to come? I've never had anyone to watch it with before."

This is what he and Molly had been waiting for. This is when Kathleen would make her move—when darkness had fallen and the noisy laser show occupied everyone's attention.

"Sure, I'll come," he said.

He delayed telling Molly until she actually asked.

"Good!" she said. "Tomorrow night, it'll all be over, and we can celebrate. Just think how proud you'll be to help apprehend someone who's been preying on men for years— maybe even your own father. I know he disappeared in the park when you were little. Is it true that you were with him, that you were left wandering all alone in the park after dark?"

He turned his head away and said nothing. He didn't want to remember that night. Molly leaned over and squeezed his hand.

Saturday afternoon, Michael took a blanket and a picnic supper to the park. The green grass glowed in the early evening sun. He saw Molly, dressed like a tourist, with her hair twisted up in a bun and her big sunglasses on. Sitting on the far side of the lawn, she gave every appearance of being absorbed in a book.

Kathleen sat beside him.

"This is so exciting!" She smiled at him, her green eyes alight with happiness.

Tears blurred his eyes. This would be their last meal together.

By the time the daylight faded and the show started, he had made up his mind. If Kathleen wanted to take him into the faery stronghold and keep him there, he would let her. So what if he died young? She was worth it. He just had to find some way to keep Molly from arresting Kathleen.

After the show ended, they sat on the blanket and talked as hundreds of other people got up and left. Finally, Michael stood up and helped Kathleen to her feet.

"Can I walk you to your car?" he asked.

"I don't have a car," she said, "but you can walk me

home—if you promise to keep my secret."

His stomach cramped with fear, but he managed a smile.

"I'll never tell," he promised.

She reached for his hand and led him off the path and into the forest. Somewhere nearby, no doubt, Molly and other agents were waiting to pounce the moment Kathleen made her move.

Kathleen's hand was warm in his. He found himself caring less and less that she was a heartless faery. She smiled up at him in the dim moonlight.

"I suppose I should tell you my big secret now. I live here in the park, in a little hut I made myself. I ran away from home two years ago when my dad hit me so hard it broke three of my ribs. I have a friend who brings me her old clothes and other odds and ends. Then you bring me lunch every day and I manage to get by just fine."

A brilliant spotlight dazzled his eyes. Kathleen squeaked.

"Stop right there," Molly's voice commanded. She stepped up to Kathleen and snapped on a set of handcuffs.

"Caught you at last," she said.

Kathleen sobbed. As Michael's eyes adjusted to the light, he looked at the two women. Kathleen held her handcuffed hands over her face and was crying too hard to talk. Molly looked at him triumphantly, as if to say, "We did it!" She had taken her sunglasses off and her blue eyes gleamed in the spotlight.

He knew then what he had to do. He reached for Molly, pulling her toward him with his left arm as if to hug her. With his right hand he reached into his pocket and pulled out the iron handcuffs he had bought downtown. Before Molly could react, the bright light had fallen to the ground, and he had her hands cuffed behind her back. She shrieked and struggled like a wounded cat. He took her keys from her belt and freed Kathleen, wrapping his arms around her to comfort her.

Molly fell writhing to the ground. Her screams became fainter and then died away. She lay there panting and staring at him. After a moment, she sucked in a huge breath of air and spoke in a barely audible voice.

"Please, Michael," she whimpered. "You're killing me. The iron is killing me." She rolled almost onto her stomach and showed the red burns on her wrists, starting where the handcuffs touched her and moving up her arms.

Kathleen shivered in his arms and he held her tighter.

"You almost got away with it, Molly," he said. "Framing an innocent girl for your own crimes, I mean. You know how you gave yourself away?"

She did not answer. He lifted up the lightweight, dull metal handcuffs he had taken off of Kathleen's wrists.

"Why on earth would you use aluminum handcuffs unless you had some reason to avoid steel?" he said. "No doubt you've noticed that I managed to procure some good old-fashioned iron cuffs."

Molly hissed, then gasped for breath.

"Your really big mistake was putting your hair up," he continued. "I finally realized who you remind me of. It was you—you who led my father away that night over twenty years ago. You smiled at me and told me you just needed to talk to him for a few minutes. I never saw him again."

"You Mahoney men are so delicious," she said. "I never could resist you. I had your grandfather too, you know. Back in the old country, that was. I followed your father here to wait for him to grow up. And I'm dying, Michael. I need you. Come with me."

"You told me yourself that faeries have no feelings," he said. "No wonder you knew so much about them. I'll call the real police and tell them where to find you. Maybe they'll know what to do with you. I can testify against you if they ask me to."

He smiled down at Kathleen, still safe in his arms. "I believe I promised to walk you home, my lady."

The End

Dragon Moon

"**I** don't get many requests to do soles," the tattoo artist said.

Darla clenched her teeth. "No kidding."

She had slathered her foot with a topical anesthetic, but the effects were wearing off, and she was starting to wonder how she was going to walk home.

"You walked here, didn't you?" Greg, the tattoo guy, must have read her mind. "Why don't I get my wife to take you home? I don't know how far away you live, but it's going to seem a lot farther going back."

"It's just a few blocks from here," Darla said, "but I have to admit a ride would be nice."

When Greg's wife Lacy dropped her off, Darla hopped to the stairs leading to her little apartment over the garage. After trying various options, she got up the stairs by sitting down and pushing herself up one step at a time using her arms and her "good" foot. She hoped Mom wasn't watching her through the kitchen window—and she was glad the weather had warmed up enough to keep her backside from freezing as she inched up the stairs.

After crawling through the door, she flopped onto her couch. She had expected the tattoo to hurt, but she hadn't been prepared for the reality of the pain on the sole of her foot. Still, it'd be worth it if it made David smile. She pulled her foot up and looked at the bottom. It was hard to tell what it was going to look like when the swelling went down.

Two days later, she had her answer. Though the foot still hurt, the design was clear. Small blue overlapping scales covered the bottom of her foot. Lighter in the middle and darker around the edges, hints of green and purple glinted in the darker borders of the scales, but the overall color was blue. After putting on her socks and clogs, she hobbled over to the main house and into the kitchen.

"Where have you been all weekend?" Mom asked. "David's been asking about you."

"I, uh, have something special to show David, and it wasn't ready till now."

"Oh? What is it?"

"It's something private. Between him and me."

Mom's tolerant smile changed to a look of alarm as Darla limped past.

"What happened to your foot? You're limping!"

"I hurt it a little, but it's already getting better. I promise." She couldn't risk Mom being concerned enough to look at the foot.

Without pausing, she continued on toward the den that had been converted into a hospital room for her little brother David.

"Darla!" His face lit up when she walked in the door. "I missed you!"

"I missed you too, buddy." She sat down on the end of his bed.

"Remember that dream you told me about last week?"

His brow wrinkled in thought. His bald head made his skin seem even more fragile and transparent than it had before. "The dragon dream?"

"Yes, that's the one. Can you tell it to me again?"

"Well, I dreamed I saw a huge blue dragon flying in the sky. He was so beautiful! And somehow, in my dream, I knew he was going somewhere wonderful. Just looking at him filled me up with joy. But when I called and begged him to let me ride on his back and fly with him, he just said 'I'm not there yet.' Do you think there are blue dragons in heaven and that they'd let me ride them?"

Darla smiled at him. "I dunno, David. But I know if heaven has blue dragons, you can ride them as much as you want. Look, I want to show you something."

She took the sock off her right foot and swung it up onto the bed so David could see it. His eyes widened till she feared they would pop, and his thin face lit up with a hundred-watt smile.

"You got a dragon-scale tattoo? That is so awesome! What did Mom say?"

"Mom doesn't know. It's our secret, okay?"

He nodded, grinning. "Are you going to get the other foot done?"

She had expected this question, had been bracing for it.

"Yes, as soon as this one stops hurting and itching, I'll get the other one done. We can pretend I am a blue dragon— in disguise. It'll be our secret."

By June, two months later, scales covered Darla's legs up to her knees. Her car savings fund took a hit, but she didn't really care because her scaly feet made David happy. She began working extra odd jobs to cover the cost of her ink. She still hadn't told her parents. She wore sneakers and jeans most of the time so they had no reason to suspect that under those faded jeans, her legs were covered with scales.

David was thrilled. "If you have dragon feet, you should have a dragon name. A girl dragon name."

They spent several delightful days discussing and discarding every dragonish name they could think of, before settling on the name "Indiglory," to emphasize the beautiful color of the scales and the general gloriousness of being a dragon. From that moment on, David never called her Darla again unless Mom or Dad was in earshot.

That evening, however, Mom climbed up to Darla's apartment after David had fallen asleep.

"Darla, you know I'm thrilled you and David have such a close bond. I would never have believed a nineteen-year-old and a nine-year-old would be such good pals. But Dad and I are worried about you."

"Why? Because I care about my little brother?"

"No, dear—because you care too much. When was the last time you went to a movie with your friends? How long has it been since you talked about taking college classes? What kind of life are you going to have left after David dies?"

"Don't say that! Why do you give up so easily? He's not gonna die! He's getting all the right medicine! I'm helping him get better!"

"I don't deny that you're helping him *feel* better, Darla. But you know as well as I do that the chances are very slim he'll recover."

Darla put her hands over her ears. "Don't *say* that!"

The next Saturday she kept another appointment with Greg, wearing a long skirt that reached to her ankles.

"I'm ready for the thighs now," she said, trembling inside.

She was a modest girl who hated baring her thighs to anyone. But Lacy had been working side-by-side with Greg on her tattoos, and that somehow made it more bearable.

The scales had been gradually increasing in size as they crept higher up her legs. She would never have believed she would think her legs looked beautiful covered with scales, but she did. It helped that Greg and Lacy were such gifted artists. Getting the inside of her thighs done was even more excruciating than her feet, but at least she didn't have to walk on them. She lay with tears streaming down her cheeks, but she didn't move or cry out. If David could tolerate what he'd been through, who was she to complain about the temporary pain of a tattoo?

She knew that somehow, her tattoos kept David going. Each new addition to her scales delighted him. They spent hours speculating on the details of dragon life. Since the first tattoo, she had read him two whole series of books about dragons, making a point to choose books that portrayed them in a positive, heroic light. They now referred to his room as his "lair," and they piled all his most prized possessions under his hospital-style bed to stand in as his treasure hoard.

That night, as she lay awake in bed with her thighs burning, she asked herself how far she was willing to go. She had once thought she would stop at the soles of her feet. Now, she often thought of herself as Indiglory rather than Darla. How would she feel about her beautiful dragon legs twenty years from now? Thirty? It didn't matter. David mattered. He never talked about his illness anymore. The dragon dream had captured his imagination—and for the rest of her life, the tattoos would remind her of her brother.

By July her back had been inked, complete with folded-up wings and tattooed spikes down the middle—except for the part where a rider might sit. Her car savings were severely depleted. But when she put a swimsuit on under her clothes, and then showed her back to David, he gasped in delight.

"Oh, Indiglory, the spikes are perfect! I always imagined them a solid indigo blue!"

At that moment, Mom walked into the room and stopped dead in her tracks, her hand over her mouth. Darla stood there in her swimsuit, her blue-scaled legs bare.

"Please tell me you just drew on yourself with markers," Mom said.

"Isn't it awesome?" David said. "She's my dragon sister now! Her new name is Indiglory."

"Turn around," Mom ordered. Her voice shook in a way that Darla had never heard before.

Darla turned around, exposing her back to her mother's scrutiny. She heard the horrified gasp, but she kept a smile on her face and winked at David.

"I have nothing to say," Mom said. "I'm speechless. I'll let your father deal with this."

She all but ran from the room and slammed the door, but Darla could still hear the sobs that echoed from the hallway.

She braced herself for the confrontation to come, wishing she could keep her parents *and* David happy. It would have been easier to take if Dad had been angry rather than sorrowful.

"I can't order you to stop defacing your body," he said, "because you're an adult and you're earning the money to do this to yourself. But I just want you to know it grieves me to think you didn't believe your body was attractive by itself. You'll always be beautiful to me, Darla, but the tattoos don't make you any *more* beautiful than you were before."

"It's not about beauty or vanity, Dad. It's about David. It's a private world he and I share. A world where I'm a dragon called Indiglory and he's my little friend."

"He *has* been talking about dragons a lot lately," said Mom. "He barely notices his physical discomforts because he's so focused on his fantasy. I can't fault you on your motives, Darla."

Now that the cat was out of the bag, so to speak, Darla could get her hands and arms done. Lacy had misgivings about doing her hands.

"You may regret it someday," she said. "I know you're doing it for your brother, but someday you're going to want to have your own life. It might be hard for you to do some things if you look like a giant blue lizard."

Darla said nothing. Greg and Lacy were a second family to her now. How could they question her when she was single-handedly keeping David alive? Back in the winter, the doctor had said David would be gone before Easter—yet here it was August and he could still go outside every afternoon, to talk and eat and smile and laugh. Whatever the future cost might be, it was worth it. Her hands were inked with beautiful little scales, none larger than a quarter of an inch across. That night, Mom cried at the supper table.

Eyebrows were raised at work when Darla showed up with her newly inked hands and arms, but since it didn't affect her ability to stock the shelves at Wal-Mart, she didn't suffer any repercussions.

By the beginning of October, her neck and chest were done.

"Don't even think about asking us to do your face," Greg said. "I promise you'll regret it. Maybe not right away, but years from now when you have children of your own."

"Chill," she said. "I'm not ready to get my face done either."

Temperatures fell as autumn progressed. During the warmest part of the day, Darla wheeled David outside to the backyard, after all but burying him under blankets and putting a thick fuzzy hat on his head. They talked about their private world and watched the leaves blow off the trees one by one.

"You're almost all dragon now, Indiglory," David said. "But you're still my sister, too. I like having a dragon for a sister. It makes me fearless."

Darla smiled. "You've always been fearless, David. I'm the coward."

He was even thinner now, and fear clutched at her heart when she looked at him. She couldn't still pretend he was getting better, or deny what her eyes saw every day: her little brother was fading away.

When the shorter days of November came, they had to give up going outside. Darla kept David busy helping her draw a map of Indiglory's home world. For hours at a time, they discussed the history behind each feature on the map. David's thin face lit up each time she laid the map out on the floor so she could work on it while he watched and made suggestions.

On December 3rd, the first snow fell, blanketing everything in white powder and transforming their little neighborhood into an enchanted dream world.

"Can't you stay with me tonight?" David asked. "On a snowy night like this, I could use a dragon to keep me warm."

How could she say no? She ran to her apartment to get an old pair of shorts and a t-shirt to sleep in. She giggled to think of having a sleepover with her little brother.

"Won't you be cold with shorts on, Indiglory?"

"Dragons don't get cold," she said. "We keep our favorite humans warm."

She climbed into the bed beside him, on the side without the tubes and wires, and carefully folded her arms around his impossibly fragile body as he snuggled next to her.

Mom came in. "What's going on here?"

"We're having a sleepover," David said. "My dragon sister is keeping me warm."

"Mom, could you please open the curtains before you turn off the light?" Darla asked. "We want the moonlight to shine in on us tonight."

David yawned. "The first full moon after the first snow is the dragon moon."

A frisson of excitement trilled down Darla's spine. *The dragon moon.* It sounded so mysterious and tantalizing.

They lay awake for some time, whispering together and watching the moonlight on the snow. Finally, David fell asleep and Darla felt her own eyes drooping.

When she awoke, the moon rode high in the sky and she felt something was wrong—not with David, but with herself. Ever so gently, she withdrew her arms from around David and slid from the high hospital bed onto the floor. Her feet felt weird. She walked over to where the moonlight came in through the window and looked down. They weren't *her* feet anymore. They were beautiful reptilian feet, covered with glittering scales and complete with dangerous-looking talons.

She held her hands out. They, too, had transformed into gleaming claws. The muscles of her arms and legs rippled under real dragon scales. She could hardly believe it. Turning to gaze down at David, she was puzzled at how far away he looked, until she realized dragons were taller than girls. She flexed her shoulders and felt her wings unfurling behind her as they filled with the blood pumped from her dragon heart. If she didn't get out of the house soon, she wouldn't fit through the door.

Leaning down, she scooped up David in her scaly arms. He opened his eyes and they widened in the moonlight. His face filled with joy.

"It's the dragon moon!" he said. "It made you real, Indiglory!"

"I have to get outside before I get too big. Do you want to come with me?"

He nodded, his eyes huge and bright in his pinched little face. He disconnected himself from all the tubes and wires and pulled on his old red bathrobe, now ridiculously big for him.

Hugging him to her scale-covered chest, she tiptoed through the house to the family room door, her long spiked tail dragging behind her. David giggled as she squeezed through the sliding door and popped out onto the patio.

"Come on," she said. "Time to climb on my back. What could be better than riding a dragon on the night of the dragon moon? The snow can't make you cold if you're with me."

She bent down and kissed his forehead with her new lips before he climbed onto her back and hooked his skinny little legs around her shoulders. Dropping to all fours, she spread her enormous wings out till they reached from side to side of their big backyard. Seething hot blood coursed through her veins and filled her fierce dragon heart with strength and courage.

"Hang on tight!" she said.

David wrapped his little arms around her newly-lengthened neck. Even though she had never had wings before, she knew how to use them. Her mighty muscles lifted the wings and then brought them down. Just like that, her feet left the ground. A few swift strokes and she and David soared skyward above the glittering moonlit world.

"Where are we going?" David asked, his voice full of joy.

"Wherever we want!" she answered, and they both laughed.

Denise Emerson lay awake in bed, worrying about David, her beloved only son. He was so frail now—he could slip away at any time. Thank goodness Darla was with him. If anything happened, Darla would let her know.

She heard a sound she couldn't place at first. It sounded like someone dragging something heavy through the house while making clicking noises. Yikes!

She nudged her husband. "Mark! I think there's someone in the house."

He sat up, alert. They heard the sliding glass door in the family room open.

"You stay here," He swung his feet over the side of the bed and stuffed his feet into his slippers.

"No, I'm coming with you." The icy fingers of fear gripped her heart, and she didn't want to be alone.

Mark grabbed a baseball bat from the hall closet and they crept into the family room, where the sliding door stood wide open. Hand in hand, they ran to the door in time to see an enormous blue dragon spreading out its wings in the moonlight. David sat on the beast's back in his old red bathrobe. His arms were wrapped around its scaly neck, and while they watched, he laid his head down against that mighty neck. The dragon beat its huge wings, rose gracefully into the air, and soared across the full moon in the cold night sky.

She should be screaming or calling out, but instead she just watched that dragon—it must be Darla, somehow—fly away with her son. Hot tears welled from her eyes and cooled instantly on her cold cheeks.

"Well, they're gone," Mark said. "Both of our babies." He sounded as forlorn as she felt.

He pulled the sliding door closed behind them when they finally walked back inside, and she said, "Don't lock it. In case they come back."

"They're not coming back."

He led her back to David's room, the room where he had fought for life for over a year now. Eight months of that time had been a gift—a gift from the dragon that had once been their daughter. The door of David's room stood open and she heard Mark gasp in surprise as he crossed the threshold. She pushed past him to look, and then held her breath.

Both of their children still lay curled up on the bed. Darla's eyes were open, and wet with tears. Her pearly white arms wrapped around the lifeless body of her little brother. There was no sign of a tattoo.

"Your tattoos!" Mark said. "What happened to your tattoos?"

Darla sat up and stared at her arms in the moonlight. "They're gone!" Her voice quivered with both grief and puzzlement.

Denise nodded, tears springing to her eyes as the answer came to her. "They belonged to Indiglory. I guess she took them when she took David."

Darla looked at David's body, lovingly stroked the soft bald head one last time.

"David's dream came true, Mom. He rode home on a dragon."

The End

About the Author

L.M. Burklin has been a storyteller and writer since childhood. Raised primarily in Africa, she wrote for and edited her college newspaper for two years while earning her English degree.

For seventeen years, she has taught writing classes to her own and other homeschooled children, and authored the Story Quest creative writing curriculum.

She has written a memoir, numerous short stories and novels.

Her passion is speculative fiction.

Find out more about her at:
http://www.lindaburklin.com

Check out her blog page:
https://steadfastscribe.wordpress.com/

Bear Publications

Bear Publications is a Christian publisher of speculative short story anthologies, novels, and non-fiction that relates to science fiction and fantasy.

We believe that publishing great stories and non-fiction works within a context of morality honors God, even when they are not specifically or overtly Christian. Yet in some contexts, being clearly and openly Christian is also appropriate. We do both.

Learn more at: www.bearpublications.com or scan with your smartphone the QR Code below:

More Titles

BALPHRAHN SERIES

FANTASY

NOVELS

MYTHIC ORBITS SERIES

SCIENCE
FICTION

ANTHOLOGY
COLLECTIONS

POWERFUL
SPECULATIVE FICTION

CPSIA information can be obtained
at www.ICGtesting.com
Printed in the USA
LVHW010127190422
716592LV00006B/118